TWELVE

TWELVE

What Can Go Wrong?

M. L. Williams

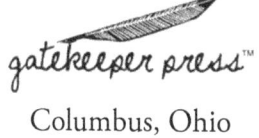
gatekeeper press™

Columbus, Ohio

Twelve: What Can Go Wrong?

Published by Gatekeeper Press
2167 Stringtown Rd, Suite 109
Columbus, OH 43123-2989
www.GatekeeperPress.com

The cover design and editorial work for this book are entirely the product of the author. Gatekeeper Press did not participate in and is not responsible for any aspect of these elements.

Library of Congress Control Number: 2021933021

ISBN (hardcover): 9781662910906
ISBN (paperback): 9781662910913
eISBN: 9781662910920

Contents

Chapter 1

"Single-file line, please!" Mrs. Taebor yells as everyone tries to cram onto the bus. "We will not board this bus until I have a single-file line!"

Everyone tries to squeeze between one another. Our bags are making this a little more difficult than it should be.

"Teagan, will you move your elephant-sized sleeping bag?!" Dakota yells, shoving it away from her face.

Teagan struggles to tame her apparent zoo animal. She pulls it out of the way and places it on the ground.

"There, happy?" she says, glaring at Dakota.

"Uh, yeah," Dakota replies.

I shake my head and put my backpack and sleeping bag down next to me. We're going on a class camping trip. I'm really excited and kind of nervous about it. Oh, yeah, which reminds me – the last time we left off I was at a dance. Believe it or not, that was two years ago and a lot has happened since...

In case you're wondering, yes, I broke up with David. I promised myself I would never ever date anyone unless I was actually interested in them; dating him was the absolute worst because I felt pressured to be in the relationship. I didn't break up with him at the dance. I didn't want to embarrass him; and he was so nice the entire night. He was definitely a good guy for someone who would like him back; he just wasn't for me.

Instead, I decided to break it off a few days later. I called and asked him to meet me at a nearby park. I could tell by the look on his face that he knew what was coming. It was such a confusing time in my life. At least, we remained friends and spoke in school and sometimes walked to classes together. We sent the occasional text message, and it was nice having him as a friend, no pressure.

Of course, being the school "couple," I was flooded with people asking why we broke up. I think half of my classmates were more upset about it than me. After a few weeks, the questions stopped, but every time David and I walked to class together, everyone wondered if we were back together. It was kind of funny but it got annoying as time went on.

Ever since the dance, I've gone to bed every night thinking about Jess kissing me on the cheek. I've probably replayed it in my head a thousand times, even though I know it meant nothing. I've had moments when David's kiss slips into my mind, but Jess's kiss completely takes over those thoughts. I don't know. It was different. It's hard to explain. David's kiss and Jess's kiss both gave me such different feelings.

I went over and over in my head what those differences might be. Was it just me? Was there something wrong with me? Was I a twelve-year-old freak of nature? I've still failed to figure that one out.

In the meantime, Jess and Dani became friends again, though I don't know if it was the same as before, or if it was weird. Jess didn't say too much. I called it, by the way…

Jess and I never told anyone Dani's secret, and Dani still has no idea that I know she likes girls more than boys. I'm such a great friend to a someone who's not even my actual friend. How awesome am I? I never even told Teagan! I love her and confide in her so much, but I wasn't going to trust her to keep Dani's secret. Can you imagine if Teagan had told anyone else, and Jess found out? She'd never trust me again. She'd never speak to me again! I cannot have either of those!

I bet you're also wondering about Jess and Sam. They kept dating, and they always looked happy. I was kind of jealous, but I wasn't sure why. Maybe because after I broke up with David the double-dating stopped, which also meant less fun and less time spent with Jess. I like those double dates.

After I stopped dating David, I spent lots more time at home and hearing about how much fun Jess and Sam were having together. That was kind of depressing. I know – David would have taken me anywhere I wanted, but that wouldn't have been fair to him. I wasn't about to give the guy any false hope about us. He was way too nice to do that.

The rest of the year was pretty normal, and I was happy when summer vacation finally started. Sometimes, school drama can be draining.

Eighth grade was the same as seventh; they should just combine the two. School, sports, home, and repeat. The best part about all of that was that Jess and I were finally on the same team, so we had a bunch of classes together. I never wanted them to end, but sadly they did.

Eighth grade was the end of Jess and Sam – but not an *end* end. They were back and forth like a tennis ball. I was there for Jess during every break-up and every time they got back together. Sometimes, it made me dizzy. Other times, it was just annoying.

To make things worse, it was never Jess who did the breaking up. Most of the time, it was Sam, and when he did it, Jess would fall apart. I think it was an ego thing for her. She hated all the questions she got – the exact same things people asked me when I broke up with David. Super annoying. I don't blame her.

They survived all of eighth grade on and off, but over the summer, Sam went away to a baseball camp and met another girl. She was supposedly a really good pitcher and quite the hitter. I guess she was because, according to Jess, she hit on Sam constantly and basically stole his heart.

I tried to make Jess feel better. I knew she wasn't used to losing a guy to another girl. But she did. I was glad to be there for her even though she did get on my nerves a bit. Fortunately, she was over Sam by the beginning of August.

And that brings me to the present day…

Jess and I are still best friends. I haven't told her that I still think about her kissing me all the time; I should probably take that one to the grave with me. Anyway, it's the week before freshman year starts and it's tradition that the newest freshman class goes on a camping trip to Camp Faye. It's four hours away from school...

⌐

There are probably fifteen buses lined up at our high school, and I can't find which one Jess is waiting at. I could text her, but it's more fun to play my favorite game of "Where's Jess?" There are so many new kids this year, so it's way more challenging. There are two junior highs in our town and the kids from both end up at Pellman High – so we doubled in size. It's cool to see so many new faces but right now it's annoying because there's only one face I care about seeing the most.

I feel a tap on my shoulder. I turn around.

"Looking for someone?" Jess is standing behind me with the morning sun shining directly into her eyes. Her shades seem to be substituting as a headband. She should have put them on to save my heart from exploding.

Two years, and I can't stop feeling like a bowl of Jell-O around her. I didn't see her much over the summer. We mostly talked on the phone and texted all day and night. My family went on vacation, then her family went, then there was the whole Sam break-up drama, my basketball tournaments, and then my mom sent my sister and me to my aunt's for a week so she could have some peace and quiet, then Jess's family decided to take a last-minute trip, and that was that. Next thing we knew, summer was over in the blink of an eye.

Jess takes her backpack off while waiting for me to answer.

"Nah, just looking around to make sure I'm the fastest so I can get to the best cabin there," I lie. "No one here has a chance against me."

"Aren't the cabins assigned?" she asks, tilting her head.

Yep. She's right. The cabins are assigned – so basically, I'm an idiot *and* a bad liar. Jess and I didn't get into the same cabin, but we are next door to each other.

"Are they?" I lie again.

"You're so weird, Marley." She grins.

Mrs. Taebor starts yelling on the bullhorn again. "All right everyone! We are ready to board! Please watch your step and only two to a seat!"

I pick up my backpack and sleeping bag and follow the line onto the bus. Teagan and I follow Dakota, watching her test out every seat before finally plopping down in the spot she'll be sitting for four hours. I turn to give Jess a look as Dakota holds up the line.

"I like this one," she says. "Teagan, sit with me!"

Teagan looks back at me. "But, I was—"

"Girls, please choose a seat!" Mrs. Taebor yells from outside the bus.

Teagan hurries and sits because she's scared of the bullhorn nag – and now I'm sitting by myself.

"Sorry, Mar," Teagan says, frowning.

"It's fine, T."

I slide onto the seat behind them so Jess and Dani can sit across from me. I put my bag on the empty spot beside me hoping no one else wants to sit there.

"That's totally going to work," Jess says, smiling at me through the line of other kids walking by in the aisle.

"Just wait," I reply.

I pull out my phone to text my mom that I'm on the bus and to avoid making eye contact with anyone. It doesn't work because while I'm multitasking, I let my guard down.

"Is anyone sitting there?" I hear.

Crap.

I look up to see a beautiful, caramel-toned girl with hazel eyes standing over me, trying to hold up her duffle bag and sleeping bag.

I stare.

She grins. "Is that a no?"

I snap out of my trance.

"What? Um, yes. I mean, no...no one is—is, um, sitting here," I say, clearing my throat.

Oh my god, Marley, you're embarrassing me.

I grab my things. "Do you want the window seat? My friends are here and here," I say, pointing to the seats beside and in front of me.

"I don't mind," she says, stepping back so we can trade places.

I stand to move. Teagan, Dakota, and Dani are watching the new girl. I can feel Jess staring at me. Maybe if I pinch myself I'll pass out. I glance at Jess and shrug my shoulders. She gives me some fake smile that I don't like. She won't admit it, but she's just as possessive of me as I am of her.

The new girl sits and tucks her stuff under the seat. I sit back down and copy her. Dakota turns around and leans over the back rest of her seat.

"You're new," she says, smiling from ear to ear.

New girl looks up and nods.

"I am – just moved here," she says, blushing a bit. "My parents made me do this trip so I could make some friends."

"Well, it's your lucky day. You found some! I'm Dakota, but you can call me D."

"That's Marley," she says, pointing at me. I give off an awkward smile.

She grabs Teagan by her hoodie. "And this dork is Teagan."

"Hiya!" Teagan says, choking.

She chuckles. "You guys are funny."

"I'm a comedian, just wait!" Dakota replies.

"You wish!" Teagan chimes in.

The new girl laughs. "I'm guessing you are too?"

I look over. "Me?"

"Yes."

"I'm okay—"

"What?! Marley's hilarious!" Teagan says, shaking my shoulders.

"She's not that funny!" Dakota jealously adds.

"Let's calm down," I say, trying not to overheat and pass out.

New girl grins. "I'm Logan."

The bus starts moving.

"Ladies, have a seat and turn around please," the bus driver says over the speaker.

Dakota and Teagan spin around and plop down in their seat, leaving me with new girl. I mean, Logan.

I immediately look away and pull my phone out to play a game. I'm also trying not to make eye contact with Jess. This is too much for me.

Before I could even open the app, out of the corner of my eye, I see a hand waving. I turn to look at Logan.

"Uh, hey," I say awkwardly.

"Sorry, I was just wondering what cabin you guys are in," she starts. "Maybe I could switch into the same one?"

"Oh, um, I think we're in cabin F or G. One sec, let me look."

I exit out of my game and open my email.

"Yep, G. Which one are you in?"

"I'm in F," she says, frowning.

"I think my friend Jess is in that cabin," I say, looking across the aisle. "Jess, are you in cabin F or H?"

"We're in F," Dani cuts in.

I glance at Dani and back to Jess. "Well, okay then."

"This is Logan," I say, leaning back so they can see her.

"Hi," Jess says.

"Hi," Logan responds.

"Are you from Richfield Junior High?" Dani asks.

"No, I just moved here from out of state."

"Oh, nice."

Logan grins. "I'm guessing you guys came from the same school?"

"Yep, and Jess is my bestie," Dani smiles, putting her arm over Jess.

"That's cool."

"Very relevant info, Dani," I joke.

Jess grins and shakes her head at me.

"Whatever, Marley," Dani says, rolling her eyes.

I smile. "Anyway, they're kind of weirdos, so I understand if you don't want to bunk with them."

Jess reaches over the aisle to lightly push me. "You're the weirdo, weirdo!"

"If you room with Marley you won't have any hair left when we get back," Dani says. "She'll drive you nuts!"

Teagan turns around. "Hey, I can't let y'all pick on my best friend!

"That's right, T!" I say. "Beat them up!"

I cross my arms like I've summoned my army for battle. Jess looks at me with her "Oh, really?" face and gives me an "okay" sign with her hand.

I chuckle, "I'm kidding!"

I would never let anyone lay a hand on her.

"T, trade me places I want to see what's going on!" Dakota cries since she's sitting by the window.

"Aww, poor Dakota," I laugh.

"Shut up, Marley, or I'll throw you in the lake when we get there!"

"You wouldn't dare," I say in a threatening voice.

"You better run when this bus stops!"

I hope Dakota is joking because I'm terrified of deep water. I think she's bluffing, but I plan on staying alert... just in case.

"She won't," Teagan says, shaking her head.

"Teagan, don't test me. You'll be tossed in right behind Marley."

"You'll learn to ignore her," I grin at Logan.

"At least if you get thrown in, you get to start swimming early," she smiles.

"If I get thrown in call an ambulance."

"An ambulance?" she chuckles. "Why?"

"Marley can't swim!" Dakota yells from in front of us.

"Thank you for telling the entire bus, Dakota," I say. "And I can swim, okay? I just get terrified of deep water if I don't have a floatation device."

"Really?" She chuckles.

"Hey, now, no laughing."

"I'm not." Logan grins.

I glance over for a spilt second and squint at her. She laughs.

"Don't worry. I'll save you. I want to be a lifeguard next summer, so you'll be great practice."

"Wow. So, I get to be your practice dummy?"

"Something like that." She smiles.

I shake my head.

"I'm so excited for the games!" Teagan says.

"Games?" Logan asks.

"Yeah, it's a Camp Faye tradition. We all compete in one big game a day – like an obstacle course, for example – and the team with the most points at the end of the weekend wins the trophy."

"Oh no, I'm so not athletic. How many people are on a team?"

"I'm not sure, I think five or six," Teagan replies as her eyes widen. "Oh my gosh! We should be a team!"

"Yes!" Dani says excitedly. "Except for Marley…"

I roll my eyes.

"Okay, but I run this!" Dakota chimes in.

"Dakota, we can't even see you," I say.

"Shut up!"

We all laugh.

"Jess?" Teagan asks. "We won't be complete without Roadrunner."

"Don't flatter her," I say. Jess got that nickname from track last year. She is a beast I have to admit.

Jess glares at me; I love that I know all of her "looks." This is her "I will kill you" face. I love it.

"Sure," she replies to everyone.

"Mar?"

I look around. "Yeah, I think I'm going solo."

"Mar, shut up. We're all in!"

Never mind my decisions.

"What if it's five? There are six of us," Dani says.

"Oh, it's okay. I'm new here. I can find a different team," Logan adds.

"No, you're with us," Teagan says. "Dani, you, and Jess will have to find a new team."

I glance at Teagan. "Damn, T."

"Well, I don't want Logan to be kicked to the curb!"

"I know," I say. "How about this. If it's five, I'll go with Jess and Dani and both teams will find two new people."

"No, Mar, we need you!"

"How about we take Dakota?" Dani says.

"Don't toss us around like we're pieces of meat!" Dakota says, trying to lean over the seat without the bus driver noticing.

Dani is so jealous of Jess and my friendship, it's hilarious.

I look over at Dani and then Jess. "Fine."

I can see the disappointment in Jess' eyes, but she doesn't say anything.

"So it's settled," Teagan says.

"Are you guys sure? I feel so bad," Logan says.

"Yes."

"Okay. Thank you." She smiles.

"Of course! We're friends now!" Teagan says. "But, I'm going to take a nap, I've been up since four-thirty."

"Why, T?" I laugh.

"I was excited for today!"

We all laugh and prepare for a nap...or lack thereof for me. I want to play the game on my phone I've been trying to start it since we sat down.

Logan reaches under the seat to grab her blanket.

"Cover?" she asks.

"Oh, um, no, I'm okay. Thanks."

"Well, if you do, just grab some." She grins.

I smile and look away. I glance over at Jess and she's on her phone. I switch over to my text messages.

Me (2:47 p.m.): someone's quiet

Jess looks over at me. I look at her and she has a sad look on her face. She looks back at her phone.

Jess (2:48 p.m.): just sad we won't be on teams if it's five to a group.

I glance over at her, instantly regretting letting Dani switch Dakota and me. I wanted to be on her team too if plans didn't work out, but I didn't want to push too hard for it. I didn't want to look so eager, so I tried to be chill about it.

Me (2:48 p.m.): sorry :(

Jess (2:48 p.m.) It's fine. I'll just have to kick your butt :)

Jess is waiting for me to look up at her, which I do. I give her my own "Oh, really?" face, raising my eyebrows. We both grin and I look back at my phone.

Jess (2:48 p.m.): oh yeah, I said it!

Me (2:49 p.m.): bye, Jess!

Jess (2:49 p.m.) :(whatever. see if I help you when dakota throws you in the lake

Jess (2:50 p.m.): oh wait, you have your own lifeguard. nvm.

My jaw drops as I glare at her. She shrugs.

Me (2:50 p.m.): omg!

Jess (2:50 p.m.): :)

Me (2:51 p.m.): i'll fire her :(

Jess (2:51 p.m.): nope. bye :)

I glance over at Logan, and she's leaning on the window with her blanket fully over her head. I look back over to Jess and she looks up from her phone at me. I remember why she's my favorite human. I pretend to be annoyed with her and roll my eyes. I finally start the game on my phone – I want to beat my high score before we get to the camp. The bus drives on, and I fall into a deep sleep, leaving the high score unchallenged.

Chapter 2

The bus stopping wakes me up. I forgot I was on a bus but the sharp pain in my neck helps me remember.

"Ow," I say, trying to stretch.

"Are you okay?" Logan asks.

I look at her. "Yeah, this just isn't ideal for sleeping."

She grins. "Not quite. You could've put your head on me, I had the window."

I didn't know how to respond to that. I could've just responded like any normal human, but we've proven many times that I'm not one of those. Instead, I just freeze with my mouth open trying to figure out what to say.

Logan grins. "Or not. That's okay too."

"Sorry, my um—"

"You're good," she smiles.

"Did you need help with your bag?" I glance down at it. "You were kind of struggling on the way in."

She drops her jaw. "I was not!"

"Ladies! What is going on here?" Dakota asks, leaning over the seat.

Logan looks up. "Oh, um, nothing really."

"I hear giggling."

Logan glances at me. "Oh we're just—"

"Dakota, we're on vacation. Can you chill for four days?" Teagan chimes in.

"Vacation?" I ask Teagan.

"Yes! Look at this view!"

I look out of the bus window, past Logan. We're at the top of a hill that looks down on the campsite. I can see mountains in the far distance, and we're surrounded by trees in a huge open area. The cabins circle the site, each with a flag raised outside with letters on them. I see G! I'm getting really excited. I can't wait to have so much fun with my friends.

I grab my things and stand.

"Thanks for asking if I need help."

I look down at Jess, "I—"

"I'm kidding."

I fake a smile. She doesn't look like she's kidding, but if she says she is, then I guess she is.

"The boys are already going to their cabins! What the heck?" Dakota yells, pointing out the window.

"No way. I'm ready to get off this bus!" Teagan smiles, rubbing her hands together.

Mrs. Taebor walks onto our bus.

"Ladies, drop your things off at your assigned cabins and then meet at the firepit. Ten minutes!"

"You heard the lady," Teagan says, hopping into the aisle. I think she's really scared of the bullhorn nag.

I take a step back to give Logan room to move out of the seat.

"Thanks," she says with a shy grin.

"No problem."

I wave my hand for Jess to go.

"You go," she says.

My face scrunches in confusion. "All right."

I make my way off the bus. There were a million steps going down the hill to the campsite, call it the stairway down from Heaven if you will. Logan looks like she's struggling.

"You sure you don't need some help?" I yell behind her.

"No, I got it!"

I watch her struggle down a few more steps. "You sure? You look like you need a hand."

She stops. "Fine. You caught me."

"I caught you four hours ago," I say, chuckling. "Here."

I reach for her sleeping bag.

"Or do you want me to grab this one?"

"Who are you? She-hulk?" She grins.

"I'm going to make y'all respect my strength," I say, dropping the sleeping bag.

"Marley, stop trying to show off your SpongeBob muscles and walk!" Dani shouts from behind.

I turn around. "It's unhealthy to be a hater."

Jess isn't amused.

I glance at her with confusion on my face. She forces a fake smile. Okay, I guess.

"You guys love bickering," Logan says as I grab her duffle bag. It's heavier than I thought.

"What the hell is in here? A buffalo?"

She laughs. "Oh no, you can handle it, remember?"

"I can!" I chuckle and lift the bag over my shoulder. "I just didn't expect there to be a mobile home inside."

"You're funny." She grins and walks down the steps.

I'm slightly uncomfortable because I'm pretty sure Jess isn't happy about me giving Logan so much attention. Logan is actually really cool and sweet. Well, as far as I know. I did just meet her. I walk over to their cabin to drop off her duffle bag.

"Marley your cabin is over there," Dani says, pointing next door.

"I know that, Dani. I'm dropping Logan's bag off."

"Just making sure."

Dani can be massively annoying sometimes.

I give her my best fake smile and head up the stairs, following Logan. Jess and Dani follow. There seems to be a lot of these fake smiles going around.

"Which bed are you taking?" I ask.

"Oh, um. You guys can have first pick," she says to Jess and Dani.

Jess looks at her. "It doesn't matter to me."

"I'll take this one. Jess you take that one," Dani says, throwing her bags on the bed.

Logan gives me an awkward look. "I guess this is me over here."

I set her duffle bag on the bed.

"Okay then. I guess I'll see y'all out there," I say, walking out. I glance at Jess one last time on the way out but her back is to me as she's unpacking her bag. I shake my head and head over to my cabin. I can hear muffled music coming out from it.

"Oh god." I say, walking up the steps.

I open the door and this wave of music almost throws me off the cabin's deck. Teagan and Dakota are dancing.

"Marley! Where have you been?!" Dakota yells.

"I dropped off Logan's bag. This me?" I yell, pointing to the only empty bed in the room.

"No, it's Casper's!"

Okay. Apparently, everyone's hyper. I put my stuff down and pull out my phone to text my mom that I've made it to the campsite safely. She gives replies with a how-to-treat-bee-stings essay, a link to a "How to hack swimming so you don't drown" article, and a video on what to do if I encounter a bear, fox, coyote, cougar, lion, tiger, or aggressive boy. She reminds me that boys are at "that" age.

Okay, Mom. Got it.

When the final safety text comes in, she finally writes to have a good time.

Of course, Mom. I'll have a great time curled up in my bed to avoid drowning, deadly animal attacks, and "those" boys. But what about mice? She forgot to send instructions for scary mice!

Teagan and Dakota make their jokes about my mom and her super long texts. In my friend group, my mom is known as the worrier. Scratch that – a *big* worrier.

The girls try to pull me in to dance with them, but Jess has me in a mood. I want to have fun while we're here; well, at least as much fun as I can have from inside this cabin. I decide Jess and I should talk. I head over to Cabin F and knock.

"Yeah?" I hear Logan call out.

"Hey, it's Marley. Is Jess in there?"

"No, they went over to the pit," she says, opening to the door.

"Oh, when did they leave?"

"You just missed them."

"Dang!"

"Hey, Marley. Thanks for introducing me to all your friends, especially Jess. She's really cute."

I freeze.

"Huh?" I say, confused. Where did *cute* come from?

"She's really, really cute." She grins. "I see why you like her."

Like her? What is she talking about?

"Yeah, she's a good friend. We've been best friends since the beginning of seventh grade."

"Oh, best friends, I'm sure." Logan gives me a look as if there's more I'm not telling her.

"Huh?"

"I really get why you're into her," she says.

I look behind me to make sure no one is around. "I'm sorry, what?"

She grins and walks out the door.

"Wait, what do you mean?"

She walks down the steps. "The way you look at her. I noticed."

I rush behind her. "I have no idea what you're talking about. Noticed what?"

She grins. "Oh, I see. No one knows about you. It's cool. Your secret is safe."

"What? What secret?"

Logan lets out a laugh – an annoying laugh.

"Play dumb, Marley. It's okay."

This conversation is going nowhere, so I head to the fire pit. I can feel Logan walking behind me, but I'm not about to turn around. That weird chat we just had really kind of shook me. I mean, sure I like Jess. She's my best friend. Why is Logan trying to read into it? Or is she?

I reach the firepit and see Jess.

"Hey," she says. "Took you long enough."

"I got a little sidetracked," I say. "Logan told me you were here."

"That's right!" I hear from behind me. I turn and there's Logan, all smiles as if she's got a secret about all of us.

Ugh.

Why did she have to be on this trip. She's really pretty, but I'm not so sure she's nice.

"Jess, I hope you don't mind that I told your *bestie* where you are," Logan says sarcastically.

Jess and I look at her, then at each other. I shrug my shoulders.

"What's that about?" Jess asks.

"I have no clue," I say. "She was all weird like that when I went to find you in your cabin."

"I'm not weird," Logan chimes in. "I commented on something I noticed, that's all."

"Yeah, that's all," I say. "Sure..."

I feel awkward, and Jess looks confused.

Logan moves closer to me. "It's okay," she whispers in my ear. "I've got good radar."

I step away and look at her. What is she talking about? This girl needs to leave me alone.

As usual, Dani has to jump into the conversation. I mean, what's the sense of having a conversation if Dani can't add her piece.

"I happen to be Jess' best friend," she says in a sing-song voice, the one that annoys the heck out of me.

"Well…" Jess starts, "I think I can have more than one best friend. Right, Marley?"

I nod. I'm not getting into this by opening my big mouth. Sometimes, when Dani's around, it's best to stay quiet.

I feel Logan's eyes on me, and I turn to walk away. Now, I want to be alone. I don't know what's going on. I feel like I'm missing something.

I start to walk and someone grabs my arm.

"Hey, Mar, slow down."

"David. What are you doing?"

"Right now, walking with you," he says and laughs. "Trying to, anyway."

I slow down and look at him. He has the cutest look on his face. I have to admit, he is good looking and does make the cutest faces. Maybe that's what Logan means about Jess.

"I kind of want to be alone," I say. I don't pull away from him. I'm not sure why I didn't. I guess sometimes he's too nice, and he can be comforting.

All of a sudden, he takes my hand and starts swinging it like we're little kids. I smile.

"David, what are you doing?" I ask with a laugh.

"I'm escorting you to your cabin, ma'am," he says playfully.

"Okay!" I say, and head in the direction of my cabin, arms swinging wildly.

"Whatever's bothering you, it'll be okay," David says reassuringly. "You know, Mar, you really are intense. Maybe you should chill a bit more and just go with it."

"You're right, Yoda," I say. "I do overthink, and I do try to control too much."

"See," he says, "if you start thinking too much, you won't have a good time, and the boys will beat you girls big time at the end-of-camp volleyball game."

He's right, and there's nothing worse than the shame of losing to boys.

Chapter 3

I lay on my bed and think about David's wise words, and also what Logan said and then what Jess said. And now I have a headache because I'm doing exactly what David told me to stop doing. He's right, I need to have fun.

My phone rings, and it's my mom.

"How are you doing, baby?" she asks. Have I mentioned that I hate it when she calls me baby? I think I have. She never calls my sister baby. She's "Ken." I think I'd rather be Mar or just Marley. Even "hey you" would be better than "baby."

"What's up, Mom?" I ask very curiously. I'm wondering why she's calling me on my vacation. Vacation? Ugh, Teagan is rubbing off on me.

"I just wanted to let you know that your dad called and he wants to pick up you up from the bus. I didn't know what to tell him, so I said it was fine."

"It's okay, Mom. He can pick me up."

She lets out a sigh of relief. We chat a little more and end the call.

Great. My dad wants to pick me up when the bus rolls into the school parking lot. He probably wants something, or to talk basketball for this upcoming year. I really can't think about it now. Really, I don't care one way or another, I guess. I have enough on my mind. No need to add to my teen angst.

As I hop off of the bed, there's a light tap on the door. It sounded like a bird hitting it. Nope, there it goes again.

I slowly walk to the door.

"Open up," I hear on the other side.

"Who is it?" I don't recognize the voice, but I'm still kind of in my daze.

"It's me, Logan. I really need to talk to you."

I open the door and walk away to sit on the edge of my bed.

"Look, I'm sorry," she says. "I guess we got off on the wrong foot. Totally my bad."

I stare at her – nothing comes out of my mouth. I want to speak, but I just can't.

"Say something," she begs.

"I don't know what to say, Logan. You talk all weird like that and say things to make me uncomfortable."

"I didn't mean to. I just…I know about you."

"What? What do you know about me? You don't even know me. Maybe we should keep it that way, so why don't you leave?"

"Marley, no, that's not what I—"

"Then what?" I cut her off.

She sighs deeply and loudly.

"Look, I came out last year at my old school. It's okay – you can too. It's not as bad as you probably think it is."

"What are you talking about?" I ask.

"I saw you holding hands with that guy a little bit ago. I know you aren't into him...or guys."

I don't know if she can see steam shooting from my ears, but she's about to get my fist if she doesn't shut up.

"First of all," I say, "David and I dated last year – we're not together but we're still friends. He's a good friend. So tell me, Logan. If I'm not into guys, why would I have dated him?"

I shake my head at the absurdity.

Logan sits cross-legged on the floor. I don't recall saying anything about hanging out, but maybe she's tired of standing.

"Look, I have really good *gay-dar*," she says.

"You have really good what?"

"Gay-dar. Like 'radar' but gay-dar."

"Logan! What are you saying? Speak English!"

"Well, my gay-dar is telling me you dated David to cover up that you're more into girls than guys. C'mon Marley! I see the way you look at Jess. You're attracted to her."

At this point, I'm fuming, but I take a breath. "You know what? I don't have a problem with anyone liking the same sex, but I am not that way, and Jess is just a friend."

"Okay," she says. "We can pretend."

I'm sure my face is beaming red. I wish she would leave me alone with this.

"I won't say anything. I promise," Logan says through a smile.

Say what? There's nothing to say. I thought Logan was a nice girl. I think I misjudged her. Who does she think she is with that...?

"Logan, I don't know what your gay-dar tells you, but I'm not like that. I think it's great that you got to come out. I'm sure it has to be better than living a lie and trying to fit society's mold."

She stands and heads for the door. "So, what about you, Marley? When will you break out of your mold?"

My jaw just about hits the floor as she leaves the cabin.

What the heck was that about? What is she talking about? My mold is just fine, thank you!

I lay back down on my bed. This definitely ranks up there as the strangest day of my life.

Chapter 4

I fell asleep to the sound of talking outside of my cabin.
I could hear the voices but couldn't make out the words.
It was probably Logan telling the others about her stupid
gay-dar thing and thinking I'm a gay person.

I wake to Dakota bursting into the cabin.

"Wake up, Marley! It's time to get this party started," she
screams with excitement.

Logan, Jess, Dani and Teagan walk in, and they all look
at me like I have a huge zit on my forehead. Did Logan tell
them about her gay-dar?

"Geez, Mar, your hair looks like it's been in a tornado,"
Dakota says.

I run my hand down the side. "I was sleeping."

"We see that," Teagan says with a giggle.

I glance at Logan and back at Dakota. I feel sick.

"I think I need to lay back down," I say.

"Mar, no! We need the life of the party," Teagan says.
"You okay?"

"I'm the life of the party!" Dakota jealously yells to
Teagan.

I glance at Logan, ignoring Dakota. "Yeah, fine. Just something earlier kind of threw me off."

"Marley, come on. Whatever it is, let it go and come outside," Jess says.

"Okay, sure," I say, stretching. I get up and walk out with them.

When we get outside, Logan moves close to me.

"Is it still your neck?" she asks. "Come here. I have something for it."

"Yes, go get that fixed! It's time to party, Mar!" Teagan says, nudging me.

I completely forgot about my neck. That isn't the problem. The problem is me being accused of liking my best friend as more than a friend. I go with Logan to her cabin. I'd rather not be alone with her anymore today, but here we are.

"Here." Logan tosses me a pill bottle.

"Are these drugs?" I ask.

"What? No! It's Ibuprofen, silly! For your neck pain."

I laugh. "Just checking."

I take out two and put them in my pocket for later.

I go over to the window for some air, and Logan follows me.

"I didn't mean to upset you," she says.

"Didn't we just have this conversation?" I ask sounding a bit more frustrated.

"Just so you know, I'm not like that," Logan starts. "I mean, I don't gossip. I'm not going to say anything. I know it's not the same here as it is my hometown. Plus, if you are like that, I would never do that to you."

I'm speechless. I look out the window towards the girls and back at Logan. I don't know what to do. I don't want to have another conversation like this – I want to run. Logan looks at me, and I know she's waiting for me to say something.

"I'm not." I smile awkwardly. "Your gay-dar is wrong."

"If you say so," she says.

"I say so."

I don't look or feel so confident. Somehow, Logan got to me. I don't know what it is, but she's so annoying with her gay-dar crap. I change the subject.

"We should get the others and head to the firepit. We've been gone too long," I say.

I awkwardly slip past Logan and make my way back outside. To no surprise, Mrs. Taebor is yelling through her bullhorn for everyone to make their way back over to the pit. Logan yells for the others to leave us so they don't get in trouble.

Jess, Dakota, Dani and Teagan take off running. Logan and I walk together in silence. I have nothing to say to her, and hopefully, she has nothing more to say to me.

We make our way over to the firepit just as the bullhorn nag starts up again.

"Please sit, girls. I said sit down!"

Really? Thanks for the headache. Nothing like a bullhorn in your ear two feet away.

I don't see the others, but it's hard to find anyone in this crowd while we're sitting.

I look at Logan sitting next to me. I'm annoyed because she is really pretty despite how aggressive she's been interrogating me. I can think that without it being *like that*, right? I mean, a lot of girls think other girls are pretty.

Too bad her personality and looks don't match. I wish I knew where she was going with all that. Why was she doing this to me?

Maybe she's going to make a move on Jess. Maybe her gay-dar zoomed in on Jess and Dani. Oh my god, I hope she doesn't say anything to Dani!

"Dinner will be in twenty-five minutes," Mrs. Taebor says into the bullhorn, scaring the heck out of me. "There is no swimming tonight! There are fun little games set up everywhere," she says, pointing around the campsite. "Curfew is ten-o'clock sharp! Enjoy yourselves tonight. Tomorrow the games begin!"

Everyone cheers uncontrollably as if they've won a million dollars.

"All right, all right, settle down," she says, waving her hands. "Remember, there are no persons of the opposite gender permitted in your cabins. Anyone found breaking this rule will be dismissed immediately, your parents will be called to come and pick you up. May I remind you all, it is a four hour drive – one way – for your parents. Behave yourselves, ladies and gentlemen."

"Lucky me," Logan says.

I laugh to myself. I mean it was funny, and she has a point.

"Let's have some fun, freshmen!" Mrs. Taebor yells.

Everyone cheers and stands.

"You know, when teachers say things like that, they never think about the kids who like the same gender," Logan says.

I give her a look. Here she goes again. What does she expect me to do? How does she expect me to react? She's deep sea fishing with me!

She winks at me, and I look away.

I search for the group with Logan trailing behind me. I pull out my phone to call Teagan, and I put it on speaker.

"Marley! Are you alive?!"

I shake my head. "T, I called you! You're talking to me…"

"Shut up. Where are you?"

"Looking for you guys. Can you see that tree with the big treehouse up top?"

"Um…um…hmm. Oh, yeah. There it is! I see it."

"Okay. Meet us there."

"Gotcha!" she replies.

"Guys, Marley says to meet at that—" I hear her saying in the background, right before the phone disconnects.

"Okay, bye," I say as the signal rudely interrupts.

Logan and I make our way over to the treehouse. I'm even more nervous because now I feel like she's watching my every move I make around Jess. We get there first, and I'm curious about what's inside; it looks huge. Logan watches as I stare at the top.

"You want to go up?"

"For sure."

"Let's go."

We climb and open the hatch to get inside. There's a sign that says, "MAX 10 PEOPLE." Ten? That seems like a lot.

"Holy crap, this is huge," I say, looking around.

There's wood flooring like in a house, a couch, and comfy-looking bean bag chairs. There's even a mini fridge.

"This is so cool."

Logan plops down and sinks into a bean bag chair.

"Well, how is it?" I ask.

"Worthy of my butt," she says with a laugh.

"Well...that's good, I guess."

My phone rings, and it's Teagan.

"Mar, we're here. I don't see you."

I walk to the window. "Look up." I see her and wave.

She looks up. "Oh, I'm definitely on my way! Make room!"

They all come up and scope out the place. Jess is hanging pretty close to Dani. She hasn't talked to me. I'd be lying if I said my feelings aren't hurt.

"We're going to have so much fun!" Dakota says as she stretches out on the couch.

They all begin their usual chatter, but I tune them out. I feel this intense blanket of unhappiness all of a sudden. I don't know where it's from. I know I'm sad about Jess, but this sadness feels more...intense.

"Earth to Marley," Dakota says, waving her hands near my face. Did I mention I hate when she does that? She can be so annoying sometimes.

I look up. "Huh?"

"Are you even listening to me?"

I smirk. "That's a trick question, isn't it?"

"Shut up. Anyway, what does your swimsuit look like?"

I stop to think. "I—" Oh no! I forgot to pack a swimsuit!

"Oh man! I forgot one," I say, dropping my head into my hands.

"Marley, don't trip, just wear a sports bra and some shorts," Teagan says.

"I guess I could do that."

"How do you forget a swimsuit? That's like the whole reason we're here," Dani says, trying just a bit too hard to sound like a know-it-all.

She's really been pushing my buttons. I think she thinks that because I'm so playful and chill, I won't snap back.

I look up, my jaw tightens as I'm about to reply. "You know—"

"Let's go see if it's dinner time," Teagan interrupts, approaching me.

"Yeah, I'm ready to go see the boys, too," Dakota says, walking toward the treehouse hatch.

I don't understand her fascination with wanting to see the boys so bad. They're the same as we left them on the last day of school – annoying.

"You okay?" T asks me in a hushed voice.

I gently move her out of my way. "Yeah, I'm fine."

"Mar, are you on your period?"

"What? No!"

"Why are you being so snappy?"

"I'm not…I don't know," I say, holding my head. I'm getting a huge headache.

While Jess waits for Dani to go down, she looks over at us. I glance down at my shoes, avoiding her eye contact.

"I think I'm just hungry."

"Okay, let's get you some food, grumpy pants," she says, throwing her arm over my shoulder.

This comforts me. My best friend being a best friend. It's nice.

"Just give me a sec, and I'll be down."

"Okay."

Teagan and Logan make their way down the ladder. I take a deep breath and massage my temple.

"What is wrong with me?" I ask aloud.

I stand to pace. I need to figure myself out within the next five minutes. I sit back down on the bean bag chair to think. I know I'm sad about the Jess thing, but that can't be making me feel like *this*. I feel like a dark cloud has blown over my head and it's raining stones.

I hear a knock at the hatch.

"Oh, sorry—Marley?!" Taylor P says, opening the door all the way.

"Oh, hey TP."

"I've been telling you for three years to stop calling me that."

I grin. "So what does that tell you?"

"Ugh. Whatever. What are you doing up here? Why are you by yourself? Are you being weird?"

"What would I—what?!" I shake my head. "What are you doing up here?"

"I told Kyle and James I wanted to see what was up here, so I came up."

"Makes sense. I'm on my way down. It's all yours, Taylor P."

"Who are you and what did you do with Marley Waters?"

I laugh. "What do you mean?"

"You're not throwing that many insults at me. It's very unlike you," she says, feeling my forehead.

I frown, looking up at her hand. "Are your hands clean?"

She jerks her hand back. "Shut up! Yes. Well, mostly. I haven't — leave me alone, Marley!"

I laugh and walk to the hatch.

"See ya, TP."

"Oh, hey, Marley! Can we fit up there?!" Kyle yells up to me.

I look down. "Probably if you suck in your gut and hold your breath!"

Kyle is a big, hefty guy; he thinks he's a bodybuilder. He's knows I'm just picking on him. He holds his hand out for me to grab as I step down.

"Thanks, bud," I say. "Yes, you can fit. You're not the The Rock just yet."

"Almost, though, am I right?"

"Yep," I say, patting him on the back. I give James a small smile, acknowledging that I see him. "See y'all around."

I begin making my way to the largest cabin on the site; Mess Hall. It's where the food is served. I guess it's not actually camping — more like camping in style. I don't even think this qualifies as camping to be completely honest with you.

A rock bounces in front of my feet. I look over to catch the idiot who threw it. Jess is sitting at a table by herself and gives me a small wave. I take the "idiot" back. I update my destination and walk over to her.

"That could have given me a concussion, you know," I say as I walk up to her.

She giggles. "Really? It was the size of a dime. And I threw it at your feet because I knew you'd be dramatic. You don't disappoint…"

"You don't know me, Jess."

Her grin fades to a slight frown as she gazes down at the ground.

"Hey, I'm just kidding. You know that."

"No, I know."

I climb on top of the table to sit next to her.

"Are you okay?"

She's quiet.

I'm getting nervous, but I'm trying not to show it.

"Jess?"

"I'm sorry for today."

"Sorry about what? The whole ignoring me thing?"

"Yeah," she says. "I was jealous."

I look over at her. "Jealous? Jealous of what?"

She pushes her hair behind her ear. It's a real weakness of mine when she does that.

"It's stupid," she says.

"It's not."

"I don't know, I just—she…I don't know."

I can tell she's frustrated.

"It's okay, Jess. Don't worry about it," I say, nudging her in the shoulder. "It's getting dark. You want to go get dinner?"

"Yeah."

We get up from the table and head for mess hall. It's a good distance away.

"We gonna walk in silence?" I ask.

"Marley you make my life kind of hard, you know."

My mouth falls open. "Me? What'd I do?"

"Yeah," she says, nudging me. "You."

"How?"

"Because you're my best friend."

I smile. "Before or after Dani?"

She looks up at me. "Stop being mean."

"Mean? I wasn't being mean. I just need some clarification on that." She gives me a quick pinch to the arm. It kind of hurt.

"I was just jealous of the attention you were giving Logan. Whatever. It's stupid."

Ignoring the pain and pinch mark on my arm, I try to hold back my smile, but I can't. Jess lightly shoves me. "Oh my god, Marley! Are you smiling?"

I laugh. "What? Me? Of course not."

"You are!"

"Jess, I would never."

"I'm going to dinner without you."

She takes off in a power walk. I jog to catch up and yank her back by her shirt. I pull a bit too hard and her body falls into mine.

"Sorry, I—"

"Mar!"

I step back abruptly, Jess and I quickly look over to Teagan.

"Come get some food, grumpy!" she yells, waving her hotdog in the air.

That cannot be sanitary.

"Yeah, coming," I say, walking to the steps.

We make our way inside and grab dinner. I stack my burger with lots of pickles and ketchup and add two hotdogs to my plate. Hey, I'm starving. I'm pretty embarrassed for turning into She-Hulk and throwing Jess into me, so I'm keeping quiet while we get our food. We sit with the group and the usual chatter begins. I tune everyone out at some point and all of a sudden the lights are flickering, signaling everyone to finish eating and exit mess hall.

"What time is it?" Dakota asks Teagan.

She pulls her phone out of her pocket. "It's 8:43. I think mess hall closes at nine."

"What should we do now?" Dakota asks. "Curfew isn't until ten."

"Anyone bring any DVDs? We can watch a movie," Dani suggests.

"Ooo, I have *Mean Girls*! I keep it in my backpack," Teagan says.

I look over from my trance. "Um, why, T?"

"For times like these." She smiles and jogs to the mess hall door.

I shake my head; she's such a weirdo.

I clean up my spot at the table and dump my trash. Jess follows.

"I forgot how strong you are," Jess says, dumping her trash.

"I'm so sorry."

She laughs. "It's fine, Marley. I just didn't know you were that strong."

"I've tried to tell y'all…but no, Marley's crazy."

"Because you are," Jess teases.

"Okay, low blow, Jess."

"Hey, you said it, not me."

I laugh and follow Jess to the door.

We head back to our cabins to shower and get ready for the movie. I was last to go for Cabin G. When I came out, Dani, Jess, and Logan were already in our cabin. Dani and Jess were sitting on my bed and Logan was with Teagan.

"Yeah…nah," I say to Dani shooing her off my bed.

"You're so mean."

"Dani baby, come lay with me!" Dakota says, throwing out her arms.

"I'll go where I'm appreciated."

I wave. "We miss you already."

Jess gives me a glare. I'm seriously not even mean to that girl. She starts it most of the time.

I sit on my bed. "She started it."

"Okay, everybody, shh," Teagan says, turning off the lights.

I don't know why, but that sends me into a minor panic. I've never done something like this with Jess, so I'm trying to be cool. My heart is beating so hard I'm pretty sure I can see it through my shirt. Jess and I lean against the wall and stretch our legs across my bed. Ten minutes into the movie, I can't focus; it's too cold in the cabin.

"Okay, what the hell," I say. "Why is it so cold in here?!"

"Okay, I thought it was just me," Dakota says, curling up under her blanket. "Come on, Dani, get a move on before my nipples fall off."

My eyes grow big. "Wow."

I look at Jess. "And you say I'm the crazy one."

I reach for my sleeping bag and unzip it, turning it into a blanket.

"I'm literally shivering," Jess says. I can see her shaking.

"I think they're trying to kill us."

"Okay, now that we all have blankets, shh!" Teagan yells, playing the movie again. She acts like we've never seen this movie before.

Now that I'm warming up, I can focus on the movie... or so I thought.

Believe it or not, I fall asleep soon after Teagan starts the movie back up. I wake to a dark room and a head leaning on my shoulder. I look for my phone, feeling around the bed with my hands. Then I remember that it's in my shirt pocket. The clock on my phone says it's three in the morning. I guess this movie night has turned into a sleepover party. Since curfew is at ten, no one can leave without getting busted by the bullhorn nag. I swear, that woman has eyes in the back of her head, super hearing, and bogey detecting radar that would embarrass the United States Air Force.

I gently shake Jess awake so she can lay her head on a pillow.

"Jess," I whisper.

"Hmm."

"Lay down."

"Hm."

Okay, talking isn't going to do it. I grab her and gently pull her to the head of the bed and lay her down. I stretch out my sleeping bag so it's covering us both. I look over at her, knowing I can't see in the dark and smile. This is our first ever sleepover. Not the best for a couple of high school girls, but I'll take it.

I roll over and close my eyes.

Chapter 5

"JESS!"

    I jolt out of my sleep.

"Get up! Taebor is coming!" Dani says, standing at the window.

I'm trying to remember where I am. The lights are bright, and I feel like I've slept for five minutes. Jess climbs over me, hopping out of the bed.

"Marley, you too! Get up! We have to pretend we've all been up hanging out just this morning," Dakota says, throwing a pillow at me.

I stretch my legs and arms, hoping to get my brain to catch up with what's happening. I glance at Teagan, and Logan is staring at me. She looks away quickly.

That's weird. I ignore it and roll over the edge of the bed onto the floor.

"Could you be any more dramatic?" Dani says, folding her arms.

"She's here!" Teagan whispers.

I couldn't get off the floor before Taebor knocks and comes in. Nothing like giving us time to answer – I'm glad we're dressed.

"Good morning, ladies," she says smiling, holding a clipboard with her bullhorn strategically placed on top.

"Good morning!" we all reply like a choir.

I sit up to look just a little less crazy.

"Team registration will begin promptly after breakfast. Our first game will begin at noon with lunch to follow. When you hear a horn sound, this means it's time to gather for the game. The next sound will be a double-horn, signaling the game is starting. If you hear this and you are not at the game, your team will receive zero points for that game. Pay close attention, ladies! Your *full* team must be present to be eligible for the games."

For a moment, I thought she was going to use her bullhorn to demonstrate. Thank god she didn't in these small cabins.

Teagan raises her hand. Of course. Teagan always has a question.

"Yes?"

"How many people can be on a team?"

"Oh, yes, each team can only have six people. Each game is designed for this exact amount."

You can feel the excitement in the air. We all know that means we get to be on the same team.

"Any other questions?" Taebor asks.

We all shake our heads.

"Fantastic. Breakfast is from seven-thirty to eight. Fuel up everyone; we have a long day ahead of us."

She walks to the door and turns.

"Oh, and ladies…"

We look her way.

"How about tonight we sleep in our own cabins?" She winks.

Ugh! The nag did a bed check. At least she didn't catch any boys in here. We would have been exiled to our homes.

"Yes, ma'am," Teagan announces. "It won't happen again."

"See to it, young ladies," she says, and off she goes.

"Thanks, Teagan. You saved our parents from eight hours of driving and years of trust issues," I say.

The others laugh.

"We should've said we needed all the body heat we could get since they were trying to turn us into popsicles," Dakota says.

I lay back across my bed and stretch.

"I need ten more hours."

"Marley, stop being a grandma!" Dakota says, charging at me.

I brace for impact.

She jumps on me to get me off the bed.

"Marley, I'll save you!" Teagan says, running from her bed.

"D, get off of me!" I laugh.

Teagan jumps on the bed and slams down on us both. She lets out a deep, loud fart.

"Oh, hell no!" Dakota says, throwing off Teagan.

"Oh my god!" Dani yells, laughing.

"Are you kidding me?" I yell, throwing myself off the bed and onto the floor again.

Jess, Dani, and Logan are laughing hysterically at this smelly monstrosity.

"We need air freshener! Open the door, Jess!" Dakota yells, holding her nose.

I pull my shirt collar up and over my nose like a scared turtle. "T, what the hell? We haven't even had breakfast yet."

Teagan is still laughing on my bed, so she can't answer.

"And get off my bed!" I yell.

"Go, go, go," Logan says to Dani and Jess. They all run out the door.

"I'm going to throw up!" Dakota says.

I poke my nose out to see if the smell is gone. I take a slow whiff of air.

"I think it's gone," I say, grabbing my nose just in case.

We finish laughing and goofing around and get dressed for the day. Since I forgot my swimsuit at home, I put on my black sports bra and a pair of black running shorts. I throw a yellow cut-off t-shirt over my bra and a pair of longer dark purple basketball shorts over the running shorts. I slip on my Nikes and plop onto my bed to wait. It doesn't take me fifteen years to get dressed like it does Teagan and Dakota. After two minutes of waiting, I'm restless.

"I'll be outside," I announce as I head to the door.

It's a little chilly out. I mean, it's seven in the morning so why wouldn't it be? The sunrise shining off the trees and campsite is really pretty. I enjoy the scenery. I see Taylor P in the distance sitting with Kyle and their friends.

"Hey, Marley!" I hear from behind me. I turn around to see David.

"Oh, hey, David."

"What are you doing out here alone?"

"I got tired of waiting for D and T, so I'm waiting out here."

"Oh, yeah. Brandon is in there like he's getting dressed for prom."

I laugh. "Yeah, they're all ridiculous."

"Well, I'll see you in the water, maybe."

"Yeah, and maybe I won't drown." I laugh nervously.

"No worries, I'll save you," he says with confidence.

David is a good swimmer. He was on the school's swim team last year, and he won a lot of medals. He told me he can't wait to turn sixteen so he can take the test to become a lifeguard. He'd be good at it, I suppose. He likes the water, unlike me. It's just not my thing.

The worst part about gym class is having six weeks of swim and having to go into the pool with my period. The gym teachers don't care if we're dying. There's no excuses. Everyone swims. I hope the high school's pool is better than the one in middle school – we're all pretty sure it was put there before the American Revolution.

I hear the cabin door open.

"Uh oh, what's this? A reunion?" Dakota says, jogging down the steps.

I roll my eyes.

"This might be my cue to go get Brandon. He was doing his hair when I left," David says with a grin.

"Please go before she gets all weird and embarrassing."

David looks at Dakota and takes off in a sprint towards his cabin. I mean, he could've been more subtle, but that works too.

"No! Where is he going?"

"He forgot something in his cabin," I lie.

"Are we thinking of—"

"No, Dakota. I don't like him like that." I roll my eyes again.

"I heard you were holding hands with him," she says with an evil voice.

"Who told you that?"

"Logan. She won't stop talking about you."

I feel a lump in my throat. "What do you mean?"

"Well," Dakota says, "she asked a lot of questions about you and about you and David and you and Jess. I should tell her I'm your best friend – not these chumps!"

"Why would she do that?" I ask, perplexed, ignoring her best friend statement. This Logan girl is really starting to piss me off.

"I think it's weird," Dakota says. "She just asks a lot of questions. Probably because she's the new girl."

I roll my eyes and yell for Teagan.

"What the hell is she doing?"

"She was using the bathroom when I left."

"Woah. TMI! Okay, never mind."

I sit on a tree stump while we wait for Teagan. Jess, Dani, and Logan came out of their cabin while we're waiting. They all put their hair up the same high ponytail. Jess is wearing a tank top and running shorts along with Dani, and Logan is wearing a pink t-shirt with running shorts. I would be lying if I said I wasn't staring at Jess and Logan. I catch myself and turn to Dakota.

"Daaamn! Okay!" she says to them.

Of course, that doesn't help, and I'm forced to look again.

"You like?" Dani takes a runway spin.

I raise my hand to speak.

"Shut up, Marley."

I laugh because I was definitely about to make a smart comment. I glance at Logan and then at Jess. Dani is looking at them both. It's quite the stare-fest.

"I'm here!" Teagan says, running down the steps.

Oh, thank god.

"Finally, stinky!" Dakota laughs.

We all laugh at Dakota and head to breakfast. On the way over, we run into a few of our friends and invite them to sit with us. I'm still a little groggy from last night so I'm pretty quiet. I eat my breakfast and go over to toss my trash. As I do, Mrs. Taebor announces that registration is available for those who want to participate. I run over to the table to let them know I'm signing us up. I tap Jess on the shoulder to see if she wants to come with me.

"Hey, you wanna—"

"Can I come with you?" Logan asks.

I look across the table at her and back down at Jess. How do I get into these situations?

"Oh, um, I actually—"

"You guys go," Jess replies.

Logan smiles and gets up. "Cool."

As she's walking around the table, I sit next to Jess.

"Why'd you do that?"

"It's fine, she's probably uncomfortable. She doesn't know them."

I look up at our group of friends. Okay, I didn't think of it that way. Jess is probably right.

"Well you can come too, you know."

"It's fine, Marley."

I lock arms with her and pull her up. "C'mon! Let's go."

"You are ridiculous," she laughs, letting me drag her.

Logan walks up to us, and says sarcastically, "Oh, we're a party of three now?"

"Yeah, I think we need three people to sign us up properly."

I realize that I voluntarily placed myself in a position to be with Jess and Logan by myself. Oh boy.

We walk out of mess hall and over to the registration booth. We're about tenth in line. There's an awkward silence among us so I try to break the ice, even though I'm completely nervous.

"So..." I say. Good icebreaker, right?

Logan smirks. "So."

Jess says nothing.

Maybe I shouldn't have opened with "so." I'm such an idiot.

I awkwardly look around, hoping someone will come save us. I don't know why it's so weird. I've talked to both of them one-on-one and it's fine...for the most part. Now, it's all three of us, and it feels like a volcano is about to erupt. This was my worst plan ever, and the line isn't moving fast enough.

"Let's think of a team name," Jess says, glancing at me.

I look away quickly before nose-cop Logan tries detaining me again.

"Yeah, great idea," Logan says, grinning at Jess.

"Okay, what about 'The Six Stooges'?" I offer. "Ooo, or 'The Cool Cats'?"

Jess shakes her head at me, and Logan laughs.

"The Six Stooges wasn't bad but it went downhill after that," Logan jokes.

"Okay, do y'all have something better?" I say, folding my arms.

They're trying to think, but I can tell they have nothing prepared. They are so quick to take me down yet look at them both – no ideas. I raise my eyebrows at them. They look at each other with disappointment.

"Fine," Jess says. "You can pick."

I smile. "I have a perfect one."

We wait another minute or two until we're at the front. I write down our names and our team name. They try to look over my shoulder, but I block them.

"There." I say, handing the paper and pen back to the games monitor.

I walk away from the booth.

Jess and Logan run up to me. "Well?" Logan asks.

"Well, what?"

"Marley!" Jess says, grabbing my arm.

I laugh. "It's a surprise. You guys will love it."

They look at each other and shake their heads. They know they messed up.

Chapter 6

Our first game is a scavenger hunt. I'm really competitive so this is right in my element. I've spent the last ten minutes planning the entire operation so we can beat the other teams.

There are thirty-two items on the hunt list, so it's going to take some time to get through it all. I'm thinking if we split into groups of two we can cover more ground in the woods.

"Okay, I got it," I say, as I gather the others into our version of a huddle.

Dakota sits on a tree stump and crosses her legs. "Let's hear this master plan…uh…master."

I glare at her in annoyance. "I say we split into groups of two so we can find more items faster."

"I call Jess!" Dani yells with her hand up.

Everyone looks at her.

"Sorry. That was really loud, wasn't it?" she says, as her face turns candy apple red.

I look back to the group. "Anyway, we—"

"How can we split into groups of two when we only have one camera?" Logan asks.

"Damn, I didn't think about that," I say, plopping my butt down on another tree stump.

Jess mugs me for saying "damn." I give her a grin, acknowledging her mug. I let out a sigh and start to think of another winning plan to win this scavenger hunt.

It's silent for about two minutes.

"I got it!" Teagan yells.

We look over. "Okay, whatcha got, T?" I ask.

"Be right back," she says, sprinting for the cabin.

"Okay, this should be interesting."

As Teagan runs for the cabin, I try to think of a plan B. I'm slightly annoyed Dani aggressively chose Jess – she beat me to it. Fair game, I guess. But, then again this strategy doesn't work with only one camera. Actually, we can't split up at all. Ugh! All of my plans to conquer this game are falling apart.

"Guys!" I hear in the distance.

I look over to see Teagan running and yelling, waving something above her head. I try squinting to get a better look at what it is.

"What the hell is that?" Dakota asks aloud.

"There's no telling," I reply.

Teagan finishes her sprint and drops three drawstring bags on the ground.

"What is—"

"Open," she says hunched over with her hands on her knees, trying to catch her breath.

I give her a strange look. Dakota and I each grab a bag. I pull it open and stick my hand inside. I pull something out—It's a walkie-talkie. Teagan always has the most random crap in her backpack, like, always.

I laugh. "T how—where—why do you have these?!"

Dakota falls off the side of her tree stump from laughing so hard. Jess, Logan, and Dani are laughing too.

Teagan smiles from ear to ear. "I thought we could use them, so I brought one for the three of us. No offense to you three."

I walk over to her, still a bit out of breath from laughing. "I underestimate you sometimes, T. I love you. I hereby appoint Teagan "T" Rodgers as team captain!"

Everyone laughs and claps. Teagan takes a big bow.

"Okay, back to business." I say.

"We can do groups of two now!" Dani says as a smile crosses her face.

Dakota jumps up. "Me and T!"

Teagan doesn't look very happy about that. Dakota did that because she knew Teagan and I would choose each other. I don't think she'd be too pleased not being a choice, so she went after mine, which leaves me with…Logan. Oh boy.

I glance at Logan. "Guess it's us."

"I guess so," she smiles. I avoid the eye lasers I know Jess is shooting at me. I'm loving this jealously. Is that wrong? Is it toxic of me?

"Okay, when you find an item on your list signal on the walkie and whoever has the camera will bring it over," I say.

"Should we give a group the items that don't need the camera?" Jess says.

I shockingly glance over at her because she's usually quiet around us.

"Yes, that's so smart," Dani says, kissing Jess' butt.

I roll my eyes at her.

"Okay, let's see…" Teagan says, looking at the list.

While Teagan is dividing the list, the first horn sounds, signaling us to head to the starting area. We make our way over and get ready to take off. I want to slip behind and talk to Jess before it begins, but Dani is glued to her hip, so that's a hard pass. I'm oddly excited to hang with Logan by myself. I don't know, maybe this is a love-hate relationship. The second horn sounds and we all take off in different directions. Logan and I run straight for the forest.

"I think I hear a bird over there, get the camera ready!" Logan says, jogging through the trees.

"Ow," I say as branches hit me in the face. "I should've worn a helmet."

Logan laughs. "A helmet? Keep up, superstar!"

"Superstar?" I ask, struggling up a hill.

"Yeah, aren't you the basketball star?"

I stop. "How'd you know I play basketball?"

"Oh, um, it came up last night. Hey! I think I see it, come here."

Wait. They were talking about *me* last night? When I was asleep? Or when they were taking showers at their cabin? I don't know if that makes me happy or nervous. I think both. I'll go with both.

"There," Logan says pointing.

I snap the picture.

"Can you see it?"

"Yeah, I zoomed in. We're good. Let's mark it off."

Logan marks it off the list.

"So, last night, huh?"

She turns and grins. "You're interested?"

"Oh no—just wondering. No biggie," I reply, lying.

"Okay," she winks. "Let's go find the boat."

As we crunch through the leaves, I, of course, can only think about their girly gossip session. I should tell Logan I want to know what they talked about but then she'll start up with her gay-dar crap again. I know she's trying to get me to admit I like girls—or Jess. I won't and I don't. Ugh, I'll just try to forget about it.

"Hold on, there's animal tracks right there," I say, pointing. "That's on the list, right?"

Logan turns around. "Yes, grab—"

"Hello? Come in Marley? Over."

We make eye contact and I shake my head. My life wouldn't be complete without Teagan. I kneel on the ground and take the drawstring bag off of my back, taking out the walkie-talkie.

"T?"

Silence.

"Hello? T?"

Dani comes on. "Marley, stop playing on the walkie!"

I ignore her.

"T?!"

"Mar, you forgot to say 'over,' over."

I look up at Logan. "What did we get ourselves into?" I roll my eyes. "Yes, T…over."

"We found a few items. D is gonna come get the camera from y'all. Over."

I look around. "Um, T? How are you going to find us?"

Silence.

I shake my head. "Over."

"Well, what do you see? Over."

Teagan is exhausting me with this "over" nonsense.

"Trees."

...

...

"Over."

"Hmm. Over."

"What is this conversation even?" Dani asks.

I'm tempted to make a smart comment, but I hold back.

"T, I'll run back and meet you at mess hall. Over."

"Tell Marley to hurry the hell up!" I hear Dakota say in the background.

"Mar—"

"I heard her. Over and out."

I let out an impatient sigh. "I'm gonna run the camera back, you keep the walkie."

Logan looks around. "Do you know how to get back?"

"I'm Marley Waters – born genius."

She smiles. "Okay Miss Genius. Don't get lost."

"I'll be right back. Head toward that stream over there to find the boat."

"Okay. Be careful."

I grin and turn around for the forest. That was nice of her to say. It made me feel a little loved. I start jogging with my head down. The bugs are really bad today, and I don't want them flying in my face. As I jog through, the path doesn't look very familiar.

"This doesn't look right," I say aloud.

I scratch my head and look around in all directions.

"Oh, crap."

I feel my pockets for my phone. I don't have it. This can't be good. Jogging with my head down may not have been the best idea.

"Teagan!" I yell.

Silence.

I don't think I should keep walking. I might fall off a cliff or run into a wild animal. I'm trying not to panic.

"What to do, what to do?" I say, looking for signs of human life.

I see a tree stump and take a seat. The good news is, it's only noon so there's still plenty of daylight left. The bad news is…I'm lost.

～

I don't have a clock with me, but I'm guessing I've been sitting here for over an hour. I want to take off and look around; I figure someone's looking for me by now. I also don't want to get any more lost than I am already. I think I could handle life out here in the jungle; it's kind of chill out here.

I keep checking to make sure there aren't any bugs crawling on me. That will send me straight out of my clothes, and no one wants to see me running around screaming in my underwear.

I accept my newfound fate of being lost in the woods and get a little comfier. I think about what possible conversation went on between Jess, Logan, and Dani last night. I don't care too much about what Dani had to say, but I'm still curious. I start picking at my fingernails like I usually do when I'm anxious. I have a million things running through my head. I also keep thinking about Logan accusing me of "liking" Jess. Of course, I don't. I mean, not like that. Jess is just my best friend. She's fun to be around, makes me smile and laugh twenty-four seven, and she's so easy to get along with. She's just a perfect human being. Okay, that doesn't help my case, but I swear I don't "like" Jess. I don't...right?

Plus, I remember at the dance how freaked out she was about the whole kissing Dani situation – there's no way I would make that mistake! Ruining our friendship is not on my to-do list. Not that I like her or planned on liking her. Ugh, I'm making my head hurt.

"Teagan!" I yell again.

Nothing.

My stomach growls, which means I'm probably on the path to death. This is the series finale of Marley Waters. I will say, it's been nice knowing y'all.

I hear leaves crunch behind me. I jump and hide behind the stump incase it's a bear or a killer rabbit.

"Hello?"

I know that voice. "Jess?"

"Marley?"

I peek over the stump. "Oh my god! You found me!"

She looks confused. "I found you?"

I'm a bit offended. "Yes, I've been lost out here for an hour. I figure you guys would've organized a search party. I see you did."

She stares at me for about five seconds before she busts out laughing.

"Hey! Why are you laughing?!"

"Marley, what are you talking about?"

I break it out slow for her. "I. Am. Lost. Jess."

She continues laughing. I'm so confused.

"How long have you been lost?"

I shrug my shoulders. "I mean, at least an hour. I think the sun was over there and now it's there," I say, pointing. "Well, it hasn't moved that much but you get me."

She falls to the ground laughing with tears in her eyes.

I smile because she's laughing so hard, but I'm so confused. I stand there looking stupid while she catches her breath. I reach my hand out to help her up.

"Are you done now?"

She wipes the tears from her eyes. "Yes."

I give her a look. "Are you?"

"Yes! Yes, I'm done. I'm sorry..." she says, trying not to smile.

"Jess, I could've died from starvation out here."

Her smile widens. "Marley, please stop before I start laughing again."

"I'm not doing anything!"

"Marley."

"Jess."

"*Marley.*"

"Jess!"

"You aren't lost."

"Well, yeah, you found me."

"No—well, yes...but, you aren't lost."

"Jess, look around, nothing but trees. Which reminds me, do you know your way back?"

She grabs my hand. "Come here."

I sigh and let her guide me. We walk a few yards away from my tree stump.

"I told you, nothing but trees, Jess."

"Shh."

I grin. Also, her hands are really soft, which makes me think about what mine feel like, and they probably feel like sandpaper.

Jess squeezes through two bushes and pulls me through.

We're at the campsite.

She turns around smiling.

I look at her with an innocent "oopsie" face.

"Let's never talk about this. Ever. Again."

"Hey, you wanna know something else?"

"What?"

"You—"

"Marley! What the hell?!" Dakota says running up to me. "We've been waiting ten minutes for your ass! Give me the camera."

I hand her the bag. "Ten minutes?"

"Yes, stupid, and we're probably behind all the other teams. Go get Logan, we need to stay together as a group from now on."

Jess is grinning at me.

"Only ten minutes?"

Dakota pushes me. "Go! Jess, go with her since she probably has a head injury."

"Where's Dani?" I ask.

Dakota and Jess point toward Dani, who's standing next to Teagan talking.

I scratch my head. "So only ten minutes?"

Dakota rolls her eyes and runs back to Teagan.

Jess grabs my arm. "Come on."

We walk back through the bushes, crunching through the fallen leaves. I don't want to be back in here, I may have PTSD or something. Oh, and I'm not convinced it was only ten minutes.

"I was by the bush looking for berries when I heard you yell Teagan's name," Jess says. "I have to be honest, I was cracking up."

My jaw drops. "Ten minutes? Are you sure?"

She puts her hand on my shoulder. "You know when you were talking to Teagan on the walkie?"

"Yeah."

"That was fifteen minutes ago."

I look at her, but then I remember I kind of melt when I look in her eyes, so I quickly stare down at the ground. I must have been pranked because the time isn't adding up. Jess teases me until we get to Logan. We find her by the river hanging out by the boat.

"Finally, I was afraid you got lost!" she yells as we walk down. "Just kidding, you weren't gone that long."

Jess and I look at each other and smile. I approach the boat and look around; it's pretty cool. Old and rusty, but cool.

"You get it?" Logan asks me.

"Get what?"

"The picture?"

Oh crap, the camera.

"Can I see the walkie?"

She hands it to me.

"Hey, T...over."

"Mar, what's up? Over."

"Meet us at the river, we need to take a pic of the boat. Over."

"Tell Marley her plan sucks!" Dakota yells in the walkie.

To be fair, she has a point. This is a complete mess, although it would've been perfect if we had more than one camera. But, why would they listen to me? Teagan is the captain!

We wait for Teagan, Dakota, and Dani to show up. When they do, Dakota and I argue about my plan sucking. After the bickering, we hurry and get the rest of the items on the list. Dakota takes off running for the campsite to turn in our items and the camera. When the rest of the group makes it back, the horn sounds signaling the end of the scavenger hunt. Mrs. Taebor sends everyone to the mess hall for lunch and then to meet back outside for the results. We all scarf down our food and run outside. Everyone circles around the podium where Mrs. Taebor is standing...with her trusty bullhorn. I wonder if she sleeps with that thing?

She starts to lift it to her mouth, but then puts lowers her arm realizing we're within five feet of her, and she can basically yell for everyone to hear her.

"I hope you all enjoyed our first game. I sure enjoyed watching you all run around!"

Everyone cheers.

"I'm going to announce the top three teams. The rest of the results will be posted on the mess hall doors, and you can check after we're done here."

"There's no telling what place we got," Dakota says, folding her arms. "No one put Marley in charge again."

I put my head down in embarrassment. Jess nudges me and grins. She's the best. I can't explain why or how, she just is.

"In third place with fifteen points," Mrs. Taebor starts. "Marley and the Gang!"

I freeze. Oh crap…

"Who?!" Dakota yells.

I slowly rotate around, they're all glaring at me. "I can expl—"

I look over at the cabin and take off sprinting towards it. I look behind me and all five of them are chasing me like an angry mob.

"Leave me alone!" I scream.

I take it "Marley and the Gang" doesn't sit well with them. Seems to me they should've thrown out suggestions. I guess I could've gone with the "Six Stooges," but they put me in charge. Once they're tired of beating me up, the name will still be the same, so it's a win-win…well…maybe a lose-win situation.

Chapter 7

I'm alone in the cabin, and it's nice. I can hear Jason and some of the other boys outside tossing around a football. I wonder what boys do at night. They probably don't watch movies like we do. They probably talk about girls.

I haven't noticed any of them checking out Logan. Usually, the new students get all the attention. She's not, but maybe she will when school starts and the whole student body can see her.

Logan is so confusing. My mind races with questions about why she's doing what she's doing. Sadly, I can't take David's advice and just roll with things and have a good time. My head is spinning and it hurts.

Then…there's my dad. Sometimes, I wish he'd leave me alone, and other times, I miss him a lot. He's another part of my confusing life.

My mom tells me these are the hard years, the "formative" years, whatever that means. My dad once told me to enjoy the high school years because once they're gone, adulthood sets in.

I think being four-years-old is where I'd like to be for the rest of my life. My only worry would be getting to Sesame Street. Now, I worry about *all* of life's streets.

David is right. I am a deep thinker.

That's why I like basketball season. It's not only fun and challenging, but also a distraction from all of my confusing feelings.

In some ways, I really want to get back home. I miss my own bed. And maybe Mom and Kendal a little.

I hear sirens, and they're getting closer. I get up to look out the window when Jess comes running through the door.

"Marley, you won't believe this," she says out of breath. "I-I…"

"What? What is it?"

"It's—it's Brandon. Oh my god, he almost drowned. David jumped in and saved him," she says as tears fill her eyes and she gets choked up. "He—I mean—Brandon, he's still unconscious. The ambulance is here."

I jump off my bed. "What? What are you saying?"

"We don't know if Brandon will live. But David jumped in and saved him."

"But if he saved him, he's alive, right?"

"I don't know. I don't know what I'm saying or what's going on. It's all blocked off and we're supposed to stay put. The police are questioning David."

"Why?" I ask.

"Be…because Brandon was naked. And they don't know if he…you know…tried to…"

"Tried to what, Jess?"

I can't figure out what Jess is saying. Why would Brandon be naked? Why are the police here?

Jess runs over to me and hugs me tightly. "I—I'm so—I don't know. What is happening?"

I don't answer and instead hug her back, as she cries on my shoulder. I start to cry. I think of David. Brandon and David are best friends. I want to talk to him, but Jess said we can't leave our cabins.

That's confirmed as I let go of Jess.

"All students are to remain in their cabins. Do not leave until you are told to do so," a voice says through a bullhorn. It's a man's voice, so I assume it's a police officer.

"Jess, you can't leave, so why don't you stay here and chill for a bit. Brandon will be okay. He has to be."

She wipes the tears from her eyes. "This is not what camp is supposed to be," she says through sniffles.

My phone rings and it's Dakota.

"Did you hear?" she says, sobbing.

"Yes, Jess is here. She told me."

"He has to be okay. He just has to be. He has to be," she says over and over.

I do my best to console her, and we agree as soon as we can leave, we'll meet at the firepit.

My phone rings and it's my mom.

"Marley, are you okay? I just got a call from Teagan's mom that a boy drowned there."

News sure travels fast.

"I guess, Mom. That's what we're hearing. How did Teagan's mom find out?"

"From Teagan, of course. She's very upset."

"We all are, Mom. And we're not allowed to leave our cabins, so we have no clue what's actually happening."

I hear the sirens again, and I know they're rushing Brandon to the hospital. My heart sinks.

"I gotta go, Mom. I'm fine, and I'll call you soon."

Jess and I stare at each other with fear. We've never lost a friend before. We don't know anyone who's died. What if Brandon dies? He just can't.

A knock on the door breaks the silence. I walk to the door, numb, and open to two police officers—male and female.

"Yes?"

"Can we come in," the female officer says gently. "We just want to ask you girls a few questions. We're reaching out to everyone here."

I let them in and close the door.

"Do you girls know Brandon well?" the male officer asks.

Whew. He said "do" not "did." That's a good sign that Brandon is okay.

"We do," Jess answers. "He's a school friend."

I nod in agreement.

"Do you know if he's had any problems at school," the female officer asks.

I think for a moment before answering.

"He's been called names," I reply.

"Bullied?" the female officer asks.

"No, our school really doesn't have a bullying problem. Some kids poke fun at Brandon...but just in good fun. He always laughs," I explain.

Jess nods. "He's got a great attitude. Everybody likes him."

"Did anyone pick on him for being gay?" the female officer asks.

My jaw falls to the floor. I look at Jess, and she looks shocked.

"Gay?" The word stumbles out of my mouth.

Jess looks at the female officer. "I—we had no idea. Do you think? No! Not Brandon."

"We are looking at every possible motive for him to be out at dusk and in the water naked," the male officer says.

Jess takes my hand and squeezes — hard.

"This is such a shock to us," I say. "Is it okay if we don't answer any more questions right now?"

The officers nod and hand each of us their cards, telling us to call if we think of anything to help with their investigation.

They leave and Jess and I break down. We say nothing about what we were told about Brandon being gay. I wonder if David knows. I've never heard anyone say anything about it at school.

Would being gay make him want to hurt himself? I wonder if Logan's gay-dar picked up on it, and I wonder if anyone in her former school picked on her. She doesn't look gay, I mean, not like some girls do. You can tell by the way they dress and do their hair. Logan looks…well, she looks like…Logan.

Jess and I sit in silence for over an hour, when finally, we're given the okay to leave our cabin. We're told Brandon will be okay, but he needs to stay in the hospital for observation for a couple of days.

We all meet at the firepit, hold hands, and cry together. Everyone was questioned about Brandon and his being gay. I wanted to talk to David so badly, but we hear he was so shaken up that he went home. His mom came to get him.

I decide to wait until tomorrow to send him a text. I can't imagine what he's going through.

We sit around the firepit for over an hour, until the sun starts setting and it gets too cold, so we decide to go to sleep.

This was the worst day ever. I'm glad it's finally over.

Chapter 8

I'm getting nervous as we head over to the lake. Despite what happened to Brandon, the adults decide we need to carry on, and that means swimming in the lake. They don't want anyone to be scared of swimming. I notice there's an extra lifeguard.

I stare at the water and think about Brandon. I did call my mom to tell her that he's going to be okay, and she was happy to hear that.

Now, we have to make the best of the rest of our trip. Brandon would want that.

Hanging out near the lake with everyone else, I'm wearing a bright orange lifejacket. I was not joking about hating deep water – so a floatation device I must have. It feels weird that we're about go in the lake to have fun, given the whole Brandon thing, but we do our best.

Dani is clinging to Jess like an octopus. I get annoyed when she does that, especially because she looks over at me all the time, checking my reaction, like she's flaunting their friendship. I wonder how Jess feels about it. We're all in a pretty blah mood, except for Dani, who seems to never quit being…well…Dani.

Logan has been getting along better with Dani and Jess today—I'll bet the scavenger hunt has a lot to do with that. It was a good icebreaker for everyone to get a little more comfortable.

"I wish I looked that good in a bikini!" Dakota says to Logan.

I avoid looking so I don't end up staring. I don't want to give Logan and her gay-dar any vibes about me.

She giggles. "You're too sweet."

"I've got this right here," Dakota says as she grabs some belly skin.

I roll my eyes because it's just that—skin.

"Oh, stop, Dakota, you're perfect!" Dani says, stroking her ego.

"Anyway," I say.

Dakota grabs at my lifejacket. "Let's see your six-pack, Marley!"

"Get off of me!" I snap.

"Come on, show us!"

"You're so annoying," I say, walking away to avoid her.

Dakota laughs. "You probably don't even have one!"

I overhear Teagan tell her she's rude and needs to stop picking on people's appearances.

Teagan jogs over to me. "You know how she is."

"I guess."

"Hey, I don't have one either," she says, drumming on her belly.

I laugh. "I guess we're belly twins."

"That's why we're best friends."

"Exactly."

She starts walking backward in front of me. "Am I BFF number one, two, or three? I think I know who number three is."

I smile and pat her on the shoulder; I walk past her.

"Hey! What does that mean?" she yells.

I turn around. "Whatever number you want to be, T."

I don't necessarily have an order for my best friends, but Teagan and Jess are definitely running a tight race. I love them both equally and in different ways. Dakota is like the little sister who gets on your last nerve, but if anyone picks on them, you get all Mama Bear protective. Hopefully, that makes sense.

"Okay, good, I'm number one."

I laugh. "Okay, then."

The laughing feels good, but also feels so wrong. I can't explain it. I feel like we shouldn't be laughing and goofing around, but the adults all tell us to carry on. I'm not sure I like that, but I guess it's what we have to do.

No one is monkeying around in the water like they usually do, and I'm happy for that.

I can't stop thinking about Brandon being gay, and if it's why he tried to hurt himself, if that's what he was doing. I wish I knew more. I'm not going to probe David. He'll talk when he's ready…if at all.

Needless to say, no one is in a water sports mood, so we find a spot to lay out our blankets. Laying in the sun is about the best we can do at this point. Later, we're supposed to be having a bonfire. We're having a normal day…sort of…it doesn't feel very normal.

"Let's connect our towels to make one big towel," Teagan suggests.

As we connect the towels, Dakota leaves to go talk to Taylor P and Kyle.

"Jess, let's go get drinks," Dani says, grabbing her arm.

Jess and I glance at each other, and I look away. I think Dani is trying to keep Jess away from me, but I could be overthinking. I don't know. I just know it's really annoying. I shake my head and continue setting up the towels.

"Yeah, you guys go," Teagan suggests. "We'll watch your stuff."

They walk off and Teagan, Logan, and I finish setting up. I plop down to enjoy the breeze. Teagan has the bladder of a two-year-old, so she runs to the bathroom, leaving me and Logan alone.

"That's so terrible about Brandon," she says.

"I don't want to talk about it."

"I didn't know him, but from the little I saw of him, he did give me a vibe."

"Logan, enough with your gay-dar and your vibes. I almost lost a good friend yesterday, and I'm in no mood to talk about it."

She holds up her hands. "Sorry. My bad."

"Okay," I mumble.

"No, really," Logan persists. "I didn't mean anything by it. I thought maybe you'd want to talk about it."

"Well, I don't."

"Fair enough. I'm going back into the water. You coming?"

I shake my head no, and she books for the lake.

"She's nice but kind of creepy in a way," Teagan says, walking back over.

I look at her. "What are you talking about, T?"

"Dunno. She looks at you kind of weird. And it's kinda creepy."

"Teagan, she's new and getting to know her way around and getting to know us. That's all."

But is it really all? I guess by saying that to Teagan, I try to convince myself. I mean, yeah, there is kind of a creep factor there, but there's also something mysterious about her – it's cute, almost sexy. Well, you know what I mean. Attractive, I guess. Mystifying. I don't know what I think half of the time. She's wicked pretty, but she can be annoying with her gay-dar and thinking I don't like boys. She fishes for information like she's trying to trick me into saying something I don't want to say.

"Sorry if I offended you, Mar. I just think she's different, and I know we're all upset about Brandon," T says. "I can't believe it's because he might be gay."

I throw Teagan a glare. "That's none of our business, and it doesn't matter. We all like Brandon no matter what. And if he did want to end his life, we all need to be there for him."

"Sorry, again," T says, and she turns away from me.

We're all on edge and snappy. This is too close to us and very real. I want to talk about it with someone, but none of us is ready yet. Maybe I'll talk to my mom when I get home. I wish she was picking me up instead of my dad. I hope he brings me right home. I don't want to stop to eat.

Jess and Dani are in and out of the lake for most of the afternoon. Teagan and Dakota wander around and come back, wander around some more and come back.

I set up a nearby picnic table while they're off doing things. Mrs. Taebor said we're having a cookout with burgers, hotdogs, pickles, and potato chips.

Soon, everyone but Logan joins.

"Hey, guys," I say, greeting everyone as they make their way to the table.

Jess looks happy to see me. Or maybe relieved. Dani hasn't let her out of her sight. She walks over and gives me a friendly nudge.

"Hey."

"Hi, Jess," I say. "How was the water?"

"It was nice, but now I'm kind of shriveled from staying in too long." She laughs.

"Jess," Dani pipes up. "Let's go hang at the other table. We have other friends besides Marley, Teagan, and Dakota."

Woah! Where did that come from? I look at Jess, and she turns red.

"Come on, Jess. We're hanging with our other friends," Dani says, grabbing Jess by the arm and yanking her away before Jess can say anything.

They take a seat at a table about ten feet away. Jess looks back at me. I shrug my shoulders and she does the same. I can tell she's uncomfortable and feeling suffocated. She's too nice to say anything, though. I wish she would.

"Marley! Come and swim!" Logan yells from the dock.

"I'll pass," I call to her.

I'm done with water for the rest of the trip. I feel like running back to the cabin and hiding in my sleeping bag. I look at Jess again, and her expression says she's sorry. I don't know what to do or think.

Dani hovers over Jess and whispers something in her ear. They both laugh, and I cringe. It bothers me, and I don't know why.

This will go down in my life book as the worst camping trip ever. What else can go wrong? I put on my big girl pants and go over to their table. Jess is my friend too and I want to hang out with her.

"Hey guys," I say acknowledging Jason and his friends. Jess looks happy to see I came over.

"Marley!" Dani snaps.

My face scrunches. "Dani?"

"What are you doing?"

I look from side to side. "What?"

"We're hanging with our other friends."

Jason hops in. "Whoa. Marley's cool, Dani. Relax."

I glance at Jess and back to Dani. "What's your point?"

"My point is you—"

"Have a seat Mar Mar," Jason says trying to break the tension.

"I'm good. I'm just gonna go back to my table."

Jess glares at Dani. I can tell she's sorry for Dani being rude but I don't care. My feelings are partially hurt. I leave and head back towards my table.

"Marley!" Jess yells, jogging up behind me.

I turn around. "What?"

"I'm s—"

"Marley! Come taste this candy!" Teagan yells from the table.

I glance over at her and back at Jess. Jess' eyes are screaming she's sorry for Dani's erratic behavior and every part of me wants to cave. I'm weak when it comes to her but Dani has really been pressing my buttons. She gets a slap on the wrist while Jess yells at me. I stare at her for another three seconds before my head and eyes fall to the ground and I walk away. I can feel tears forming in my eyes; my chest feels tight. I want to break down. I know walking away from her has hurt her feelings. I continue my path and make my way over so I can taste Teagan's special candy.

Mrs. Taebor brings over the burgers and hotdogs and grills them for us. We gobble them down like we haven't eaten in a week. She announces that counselors will be available to talk with us tomorrow if we feel we need someone to talk to about what happened with Brandon.

For someone so snappy, the bullhorn nag shows us she does have a sensitive side. Who knew?

⌇

"There's enough for everybody!" Mrs. Taebor says through her bullhorn. After a short game of volleyball, everyone rushes to the tables for their sticks and s'mores. I grab four sticks for me, Teagan, Dakota, and Logan. Dani and Jess aren't with us.

I hand them out, and we make our way to the fire.

"Here," Teagan says, handing us the graham crackers.

"Yum," I say.

"I've never made one of these before," Logan says, grinning. "I've only seen people make and eat them in movies."

"You've been missing out, girl," Dakota says, handing us the chocolate and marshmallows. "I'm going to the front before it gets too crowded."

"Ooo, me too," Teagan says, following.

"Looks like it's just us again," Logan says, smirking. "You wanna show me how to work these things?"

"Sure, rookie," I joke.

I lose Teagan and Dakota, so we find a random spot by the fire and sit down on a log.

"Okay, so this is what you do to make the perfect s'mores," I say, shoving the stick through the marshmallow. "You're going roast the marshmallow in the fire and let it catch on fire for a few seconds."

Her eyes widen. "On fire?!"

"Trust me. Here, watch."

I put the marshmallow-on-a-stick into the fire. I twist it around a bit and pull it out while it's still on fire.

"Oh my god, what do you do?" Logan panics.

"Blow it out."

"That flame is huge!"

"Well, blow it out!"

She hesitates and blows on the marshmallow.

"What is that?" I ask, laughing. "You blow like a four-year-old."

She grins at me and blows harder. The fire goes out and we're left with a burnt marshmallow.

"I'm so sorry. Oh my god, it's totally black."

"Yeah, it's a little toasted," I say, chuckling.

"Here, hold this." I hand her the stick with the burnt marshmallow.

I poke another stick through another marshmallow place it in the fire for a few seconds before pulling it out. While it's burning, I look at Logan and fire is bouncing off her eyes as she's looking back at me. And...the nerves are back. I blow the fire out gently and present the perfectly roasted marshmallow. I grab her graham crackers and chocolate and smash it together like a sandwich.

"Brace yourself," I say, grinning.

She grabs the s'more and bites into it. I'm smiling because I know it tastes like heaven.

"Oh my god," she says as crumbs fall into her lap. "How have I never had one of these?"

"Yeah, you may not be American."

"Shut up!"

I laugh and take the burnt marshmallow. It's not that burnt, but I wanted her to have the perfect s'more and this one was just a little on the crispy side. I think I'll manage.

"So," Logan says.

I'm staring at the fire to avoid looking at her. "So..."

"You're not as bad as Dani makes you out to be."

I look over, confused. "I don't know, lately she's been kinda crusty to me."

"She's clearly jealous."

"Jealous?"

"Yeah, of you and Jess."

My heart starts beating fast. "Huh?"

"Not like that. We've already established it's not like *that*," she says, nudging me. "Your friendship."

"Oh. Yeah, I think so too."

There's an awkward silence.

"Can I tell you something that might make you uncomfortable?"

I can feel my body overheating. What is she about to say? I don't like when people suddenly have things to tell me or ask me. I always plan for the worst.

"Okay, sure."

I can tell she's kinda nervous to say what she has to say.

"Um…"

Her leg begins shaking. She's nervous, but I think I still have her beat. I think my armpits are sweating.

I look at her as she hesitates.

"See, that right there is the problem…"

I'm confused. "Wait, what?"

"You."

My heart stops. I have to look at her or I look like a psychopath avoiding eye contact.

"Me?"

"Yes."

"Wha—"

"There you guys are!" Teagan says, running around the fire.

I don't know if I'm thankful or pissed that Teagan shows up.

"Where's D?" I ask, pretending the conversation with Logan didn't just happen.

"She ran off," Teagan says, sitting on the ground. "Where's Jess and Dani?"

I shrug my shoulders. "I have no idea."

"There's some talk about a huge game of hide and go seek. Y'all wanna play?"

I hop up quickly. "Oh, yes! Sign me up!"

"Sure," Logan replies.

I avoid looking at her. I don't know what to say about what she didn't have a chance to tell me, so now I'm awkward Marley all over again.

"Yes!" Teagan says excitedly. "Let's go cats!"

"Cats?" I ask.

"I don't know, let's go!" She pulls me by the arm.

As we leave the fire pit, we hear cheering. I'm not sure what's happening, but as I'm looking, I see Jess and Dani having the time of their lives with their friends. Cool.

"Marley!" Jason yells over to me.

Oh, dear god, please not right now.

This causes everyone in their group to look our way. We have no choice but to walk over. I take a deep breath. I don't feel like dealing with Dani.

"What's up, Jason?" I ask, avoiding eye contact with Jess.

"You guys joining the hide and seek?"

"Yeah, we were going—"

"Marley Waters!"

What the hell is happening to me tonight? I didn't know I was the star of the show. We all look to the left. It's Taylor P strutting over with her posse.

"Um.. yes?"

"We need to talk!" she says, glancing at Logan.

I glance at Logan, then Jess, then back to Taylor P. "About?"

"Whatever you have to say, you can say it," Teagan says.

"Oh, I don't think you want me to say this," she says.

Say what? I don't know what she's talking about, but it can't be good. I know my face has turned red from embarrassment. We draw a crowd, and Dakota makes her way back and pushes herself to the front.

"What the hell is going on here?" she asks.

"I don't know," I reply. "Taylor P has something to say, apparently."

"Just *be careful*, Marley," Taylor says, glancing at Logan again.

I frown. "Why do you keep looking at her?"

Dakota chimes in, "Lo Lo is off limits!"

Lo Lo? Anyway…

Teagan is watching the drama unfold. I should grab her some popcorn for the action.

"I have an inside source that gave me some info."

"On Logan? Or me?" I ask.

"Her."

"*Her* name is Logan," Dakota says aggressively.

"What about me?" Logan asks.

"You don't want me to say," Taylor P replies.

When I get pissed off my body begins to tremble. It's doing that now.

"Say it!" someone in the crowd says. "Don't be a wuss!"

I look at Logan. "We can go."

"Yeah, let's go before they piss me off!" Dakota says, staring everyone down.

This is when Dakota comes in handy. Before we walk away, I step into Taylor P's face.

"You're being a bitch," I say and walk away with Teagan, Logan, and Dakota.

"She called you a bitch!" I hear a guy yell out behind us.

The crowd is adding fuel to this fiery situation, yelling, "Ohh!"

As we walk away, Taylor P makes an announcement for everyone to hear.

"Logan's a lesbian!"

The crowd goes silent. All four of us freeze mid-step. I turn around and look at Taylor P. I glance at Jess, who's staring directly at me.

"Did she just—oh, hell no!" Dakota says, powerwalking toward her.

I jog to catch her. "D, no!"

"No, screw that, Marley!"

"I got it," I say.

I walk up to Taylor P. "You feel all cool now?"

"I—"

"I, what?" I say. "How stupid are you? Especially with what just happened to Brandon last night? Plus, you don't know if she's comfortable being outed, and you just told the entire world. For what? Because some dumbass boys made a joke?"

Logan walks up to me. "Marley, it's okay, let's just go."

I pull away. "No, it's not okay!" I yell. "That was so wrong of you, Taylor! You don't know her background or who her family is. And whoever told you is just as low."

She's staring at me like I'm about to punch her in the face. I thought about it, but I don't fight.

"And so what if she likes girls! You jealous?" Dakota asks, rolling her neck. "This ain't 1942!"

I make a mental note that Dakota is okay with Logan liking girls. Not that it matters to me or anything.

"Don't talk to us. Don't even look at us," I say. I grab Logan by the arm and walk away.

"Marley and Logan are gay together!" another boy shouts. "Wait, no, they're all gay together!"

"Who said that?!" Teagan yells.

"T, ignore them. Let's go." I say, pulling her away.

We take off walking to grab our things. I can't believe Taylor P. did that, especially after what happened to Brandon. I have a feeling that's what provoked it. Taylor P and Kyle did pick on Brandon a lot. I just thought they were joking around.

"Wait!" I hear behind us. Dani and Jess run over. "Room for two more?" Dani asks.

I look at them suspiciously. "You might be called gay if you hang with us."

Dani chuckles. "Better than hanging out with them. Are you okay, Logan?"

"Oh my gosh, yes, are you okay, Mami?" Dakota says.

Mami? Okay, D is getting out of hand with the nicknames.

"No, yeah, I'm fine. I've been out — just not here. I don't know what it's like here, so I haven't said anything. That wasn't really the plan, though. My old school didn't act like that."

"Screw those guys! They're just jealous that you can be yourself while they hide behind their little pee pees," Dakota replies.

We all laugh.

"Hey!"

We turn to see a crowd walking up to us.

"You guys down for some gay-together hide-and-seek?" Jason asks.

A smile lights up my face. I guess most of my classmates aren't assholes. This is a relief, for Logan, of course.

"Hell, yeah!" Teagan screams.

We all cheer as loud as we can. I glance at Logan and see a big smile cross her face, knowing that she's accepted.

"You're it, Jason!" I yell and take off toward the cabins.

"Oh, come on!" he yells.

Everyone runs back to the campsite to hide. I think it's safe to say my classmates don't mind being gay together. I only wish Brandon knew that.

Chapter 9

The day starts with a counselor coming to talk with us about what happened to Brandon. First, she addresses us as a group, then we all get to talk with her one-on-one. I didn't say too much, but I wanted to. It was my first time talking to a counselor, other than when my parents divorced. And that was different. For one, I was a lot younger, and Dad didn't almost die.

The whole Brandon being gay thing was the elephant in the room. It was very much there, but nobody wanted to talk about it.

My mom called to tell me that Brandon is getting released from the hospital tomorrow, but that he's transferring to a private school. I guess she talked to his mom. I'll miss seeing Brandon at school, but I can call and text him as long as he keep the same phone number.

I think there's more to everything than what we're told. I hope he really didn't try to take his life. Mom did say David is okay. He called her. I think it's funny, but Mom really likes David.

After talking to Mom, I sent David a text to let him know I'm here if he wants to talk. I do want to be a friend to him and be there for him. He was definitely there for me enough times!

I walk outside and watch everyone play tag while I climb into the treehouse. I sprained my ankle last night playing hide-and-seek, and I don't want to hurt it even more before the start of school next week – which also means high school basketball practice begins. I want to make the varsity team, so no more stupid moves for me. It sucks, but I'm enjoying this time just watching my friends have fun together. God, am I turning into my grandmas?

I feel better knowing we all heard and spoke to the counselor. I'm also feeling a sense of hope knowing my friends are okay with Logan being into girls. I don't know, I'm just glad they weren't freaked out about the whole thing. I mean, I've never had a problem with someone liking the same gender – it's so not cool how society turns it into the worst thing in the world.

Knowing Brandon might be gay means I know two people who like the same gender. They aren't alone, which is amazing. I wish Brandon and Logan had more of a chance to talk. Maybe things would have turned out differently.

I wonder if Brandon felt different, like there was something wrong with him. Did he struggle with his sexuality? Maybe something bad happened. I want to cry for him, but I also want to stay positive.

I check my phone to see if David texted me back. He hasn't, but maybe I don't have service up here. The woods can be a hard place to get a good signal.

I didn't really sleep well last night. I have too much on my mind. Brandon really occupies a lot of my awake time. And Logan, especially after last night.

I think she might be into me. I can't read her that well. And what if I'm into her? Am I gay? I ask myself this question over and over. Logan is beautiful. Teagan is right, though. She does have that creep factor. The way she watches me and some of the things she says freak me out. But, part of me likes it...all of it.

I think I get how Brandon was feeling.

Teagan runs below the treehouse, gasping for breath.

"You good down there?" I ask.

She holds up her index finger.

"T, are you running from Freddy Krueger? Why are you so out of breath?"

"Sorry, Mar," she says, resting her arm on the ladder. "Make room! I'm coming up."

I slide over a few inches so she could fit next to me. She climbs up the ladder and plops her body on the treehouse floor like a wet towel.

"T, what the hell? Are you trying to kill us?"

She laughs. "This thing isn't going anywhere!"

I look around to make sure everything in this bad boy is still nailed in tight.

"I guess. What's up?"

"I figured you were bored up here by yourself."

"Not really...enjoying the view."

"Oh."

"Yep."

We sit in silence, watching our classmates run around. I look over by the mess hall. Jess is playing what looks like Jenga with some of her other friends. I can't help but to be fascinated by her. I have never met a more perfect human being than her. Her smile, her laugh, her personality...is all so...contagious. *Especially* her smile. I'm trying really hard to suppress how I feel about her, but it's impossible. I think I've felt like this since the day I met her.

Actually, I know I have.

Another secret to take to the Marley grave.

"So you cool with Logan, ya know, liking girls?"

I release myself from Jess' hypnotic effects.

"Does it make you uncomfortable or something?" I ask.

"No, I think it's pretty cool," Teagan says.

"Cool?"

"Yeah, she adds a little spice to the group. And, if it's true about Brandon, well, he's really cool too," she says. "I like some of the things the counselor said."

"I liked it all," I say, and I shake my head. I love how Teagan isn't judgmental. She'll comment on a situation, but she doesn't obsess or fantasize over it like Dakota. I mean Teagan is pretty special herself. Maybe I should tell her how I feel. I'll never tell her or anyone about Jess, but maybe I can tell her that I may be attracted to girls...

"Hey, T..."

"Hey, Mar."

"Why?" I laugh. "Anyway, um..."

"Oh, Mar! I forgot to tell you, we're going to the zipline after lunch instead of tonight. You think you can do it?"

I look at my ankle and perform circular motions to check for pain. "I think so—it doesn't hurt that much now. I'll use my left foot if I need to brake."

"Yes!" she exclaims and hugs me tight. "This trip wouldn't be the same without you."

I struggle to talk. "T, I'm not dying!"

She releases the hold. "I know, you just...you make the group, *the group*. Ya know?"

"No, *you* make the group, *the group*." I smirk.

We laugh and go back to watching a game of tag. Dakota is kicking the boys' butts, shoving them to the ground. Good ol' D. I look for Logan, but I don't see her. I begin scanning everywhere, as far as I can see from up here—nothing.

"I'm gonna run to the bathroom," I say.

"Okay, I'm gonna go get back in the game," T says.

"You need me to bring you your inhaler?" I ask, climbing down.

"Mar, I don't have asthma!"

I step off the last ladder. "Fooled me!"

"Shut up!"

I laugh and head for the cabin. As I'm making my way, I pass the table Jess is playing Jenga at. I give her a soft smile and keep moving. I have to start practicing treating Jess like a "normal."

Ha. Who am I kidding?

I try to avoid Dakota on the way over, but she sniffed me out.

"Marley! Where are you going?" she yells.

"I have to pee," I say, continuing my walk.

"Come play! We'll go easy on you."

"What? No! Are you crazy? We start basketball practice next week!"

"Ugh. Lame!"

Yes, I'm so lame for wanting to preserve my ankle for something more important than a game of tag. I roll my eyes and continue walking. As I approach the cabins, I take a look behind me to see if anyone is paying attention. They all seem pretty busy, so I try my best to power walk up Cabin F's steps, dragging my bum ankle.

I knock.

I peek over my shoulder to double check no one's watching. Looks clear.

Logan opens the door.

"Hey, why are you in here?" I ask.

"Just tired."

My eyebrows raise. "Tired?"

"Mhm."

"You sure?"

"What else would it be?"

"I mean, I don't—nothing, I guess."

Not like last night didn't happen or anything...

"Okay."

That doesn't sound convincing enough for me. I open the screen door. "All right, let me in."

She tries to stop me. "Marley!"

I squeeze by and trip inside, slightly tweaking my ankle again. I hobble over to Jess' bed. I take off my shoe and massage my ankle.

"Ow."

"Are you okay?" she asks, standing suspiciously. She glances at the bathroom door.

"Yeah. Never mind me. Are you?"

"Yes, Marley. I'm fine."

"Okay, I just—"

"Can we talk at lunch?" she says, glancing at the bathroom again.

Oh, maybe she needs to go. When you gotta go, you gotta go.

"Okay, sure," I say, hopping off the bed.

I walk to the door and open it. I look down and notice I don't have on my other shoe, so I go back for it. The screen slams shut.

I look back with an "oopsie" face. "Sor—"

"Is she gone?"

My head swings toward the bathroom and Dani is peeking through the doorway. She stares at me as if I just caught her wearing days-of-the-week underwear that she still wears from when she was a kid. The room falls silent. Mass discomfort sets in, in three…two…one…

I glance at Logan, who's already staring at me. My eyes drop to the ground. I don't know why this is so awkward; it is Logan and Dani's cabin, after all, but both their demeanors are way weird.

"Well, I'm gonna go," I say awkwardly. I grab my shoe and limp back over to the door. I look back at them once more.

I push my way through the cabin doorway and hobble down the steps. That wasn't weird at all. Are they…? No, no way!

As I walk back, Teagan and Dakota are still playing tag. This may be the longest game of tag I've ever witnessed. They're too far away, so they can't slow me down. Jess is alone at her table and she's putting the Jenga blocks away.

"Loser puts them up?"

She lightly pushes me. "Very funny."

"You wanna play one game with me?"

"Fine. Loser gives up their s'more tonight."

My eyes widen. "Whoa there, cowgirl!"

"You scared?"

The competitiveness in me is breaking through. I can't let her think she's already won this.

"S'more and pillow."

"Pillow?"

"Yep. Pillow. You should have a proper neck twinge in the morning."

She laughs. "You're insane."

I hold my hand out for her to shake. She squints her eyes, thinking about her next move in this deal. I smile, staring into her brown eyes. She's killing me softly.

"Fine."

My large smile gives away my satisfaction that I won this negotiation. We set up the blocks like it's the championship game of an international Jenga tournament.

"Who goes first?" I ask.

"Me."

I laugh. "You know what, go for it."

She carefully slides out her first block and places it on top. I do the same. We go back and forth for a few seconds.

"Have you seen Dani? She said she was running into mess hall for drinks. It's been almost thirty minutes."

I pause and glance at her. "Mess hall?"

Mess hall must mean cabin in a different language because Dani is nowhere near it. Does that mean...?

"Yeah, I don't think she got lost, right?"

I look next to us and point to the big "Mess Hall" sign hanging from the building.

"Jess, how?" I chuckle.

"Maybe she grabbed a snack and sat down to eat it."

I look over toward the cabins. I start power-thinking about the situation. Why would Dani lie about going to the mess hall to go back to the cabin? Why did she ask Logan if I was gone? Why was Logan acting weird? Why was Logan suspi—?

No way!

I freeze and look back at the game hiding the fact that I've just unraveled that whole situation in my head. Jess slowly wiggles a piece loose that clearly wasn't ready to come out.

"I can picture your pillow on my bed right now."

She ignores me as she focuses. She continues to wiggle at a pace that would make a snail impatient. I lean in to see if she's going to pull it off.

She does.

She sets the piece on top and taunts me with her facial expression.

"Wow," I say, shaking my head.

She grins. "Go ahead."

I rub my hands together. "Okay, let's do this." I reach for a block and begin to pull. I'm inching it out...

"Marley!" Dakota yells in my ear.

I jerk, causing the tower to fall. As the pieces slam against the table, I throw my head back.

"Noo!" I yell. I look at Dakota. "Do you hate me?"

"No, I just wanted to scare you. I didn't think you'd be such a klutz."

I place my hand on my forehead and shake my head. Who wants to sleep with no pillow? Oh no, I lost my s'more too!

Dakota screams as Jason runs toward us. She climbs over the table and takes off running because tag never ends.

"Wow," I say.

Jess is smiling from ear to ear. Whatever, I let her win. Okay, I didn't, but my plan was to let her win. Jess loves beating me in anything we do; it makes her feel good, and I'd do anything to make her happy. If I told her, she wouldn't believe me; she'd say I'm just saying that because I lost. I guess this time I actually did lose.

It's almost lunchtime, so we pack away the blocks.

"Hey, guys." Dani says walking up to the table. I look around for Logan. I don't see her. My eyes narrowed as I looked back at Dani. She doesn't make eye contact with me. I decide to play into the situation at hand.

"Sup? Have you seen Logan? I haven't seen her in a while."

Jess and I continue picking up the Jenga blocks. I know I have Dani in a corner. If she lies she's suspicious, if she doesn't then she lied to Jess. Ugh. This might actually be really mean of me. This is so not like me. It may be a little jealousy.

"Oh, yeah, I saw her," she replies.

Jess glances up. "Is she in the mess hall already?"

I instantly feel bad that I did this. Dani and I made up last night and put an end to our rivalry, mostly because of what happened to Brandon and realizing that friendship is more important than anything, so here I am being a jerk. I change the subject.

"Jess, let's double or nothing after lunch."

"You can't double or nothing a pillow, Marley," she says, patting me on the shoulder. "Let's go eat."

I smile and grab the Jenga box. I glance at Dani to signal that I'm done with my childishness – but I'm watching her.

It's not confirmed, so I can't assume they're into each other. I kind of thought Logan might have been into me after what she was preparing to tell me last night, but maybe I'm wrong.

We leave the table with my battered ego on it and head inside for lunch.

Chapter 10

After lunch everyone goes to change for ziplining. Jess and I are already dressed so we're sitting around the firepit waiting for them. Knowing Teagan and Dakota, they'll take thirty-minutes to find the right outfits. Dakota tries a little too hard to dress to impress. She and Teagan even go so far as to use perfume like we're not on a camping trip. I want to be annoyed, but I can't say I've never done that for a certain someone. Ugh, fine, I won't be a hypocrite, but I'll bet Teagan is going to draw bees and mosquitoes with her pharmacy bought bottle.

"How long do you think they'll be?" Jess asks.

"We may be here a while. Get comfortable."

She looks back toward the cabins. "I want to show you something."

My eyes widen.

"Just come on," she says, grabbing my hand.

I relinquish my authority and let Jess drag me away from the firepit. I have no idea where she's taking me and I don't care. I'm excited for whatever is happening because it's just us. Dani is finally distracted enough to let Jess be on her own. I've barely gotten a word out to Jess during this entire trip without Dani squeezing herself in.

"So where exactly are we going?" I ask, stepping over branches.

"You'll see."

"As long as you're not about to murder me."

She looks over her shoulder. "You really are the most dramatic person I know."

I chuckle. "But you love me."

"I do."

I should know by now not to look too deep into Jess' words, but the gaga fool in me can't help it. Those two simple words make my heart glow as bright as the marshmallow I lit on fire last night…maybe brighter.

"We're almost there."

I'm still letting her drag me through the trees. When has she had the time to come out here? I can hear running water, this makes me nervous.

"Uh, Jess?"

She lets go of my hand and turns around. "Yes?"

"That water sounds ferocious."

She smiles. "Trust me, Marley."

If she were anyone else, I'd pull a U-turn faster than her next breath. I sigh and continue walking. I'm convinced this girl can lead me straight to my death. We continue walking for another twenty yards or so. She pulls back one last branch and it's a view of the mountains. There's a waterfall directly across from us that looks absolutely gorgeous and terrifying.

"Whoa," I say, embracing the view.

"Nice, right?"

"How'd you find this place?"

"Jason brought me and Dani yesterday. He's been here with his family before. He told us to bring only the people we trust to this spot because people have gotten hurt."

Terror overtook my face. "I'm sorry, what? Hurt?"

"That's what he said. I know after what happened to Brandon this probably isn't the coolest place to bring you, but I wanted you to see."

"Wow, you'd send me out there to see what the drop-off looks like so I can lose my balance and topple to the bottom? Some friend you are!" I joke, nudging her.

She laughs. "No, I wouldn't let you go look. Now, sit down."

My eyes narrow. "Fine. Only because you wouldn't let me do it."

I sit on the ground, extending my legs out. Jess follows but crosses hers. We sit in silence, soaking in the view. For the first time on this trip, I feel at peace. No Dakota running around like a chicken with its head cut off, no Dani shadowing Jess, and no Logan bugging me with her gay-dar. Just me and my best friend.

"This trip has been…something," she says, picking up a leaf to break apart.

"*Something* is a word," I reply, grinning.

"We've been on quite the roller-coaster. And poor Brandon. I'm so heartbroken. I'm really glad it was you with me when the police came."

"Yeah, it's sure been a strange week so far," I say.

"I know, and I feel like we've been in this weird fight, but not really a fight."

Well, if we look back, Jess has been flaunting her jealousy since we boarded the bus. This can't be my fault this time.

She continues. "You hurt my feelings last night."

My expression dulled. "When?"

"At the lake."

"When I walked away?"

Tears filled in her eyes. "Yeah."

Ugh. Jess, this isn't fair. You can't be the sad one. I'm the victim here!

"I've been upset because you've been letting Dani get away with rude comments about me. It's not fair, Jess."

"You feel like that?"

"Well…yeah," I begin. "She makes these rude comments and as soon as I try to answer, you shut me down." I quickly look over to her and she looks defeated. I feel bad but I also think we need to talk about it, so I refuse to back down.

"I didn't know you felt that way. I usually give you *both* a 'mom stare' to cut it out. I don't like how much you guys bicker with each other."

"Jess, it's not me!"

She glares at me. "You two use to be civil with each other, like at seventh-grade track."

Yeah, we were civil until a certain someone laid a juicy one on her. Now she's hypnotized Dani and she's become obsessed, shooing anyone who tries to get too close. As much as I'd like to say this to Jess, I hold my tongue.

"I don't know Jess—I think she doesn't like me anymore."

"Yes, she does."

I roll my eyes. "Okay, sure. Let's pretend."

"Well, for what it's worth, I'm sorry I hurt your feelings. I'll do better."

"See. That's all I ask for."

She playfully pushes me to the ground. "I take it back!"

"No, I called no take-backs!"

We playfully fight for what feels like an hour but was only a few seconds. I hear leaves crunching behind us. As I'm lying on the ground with Jess hovering over me, I tilt my head back to see who it is.

I'm sure you can take one guess who.

"There you are," Dani says, walking up with her arms folded.

My smile vanishes into a frown. Of course she shows up. Right on time. I was almost worried she'd miss her shift. Notice how she doesn't acknowledge me? Yes, Jess, she's my number one fan.

She continues, "We're ready to go to the zipline."

Jess pulls away from me. "Okay."

Dani gives us both the meanest glare and walks away.

"Yes, she loves me so much," I say.

Jess looks down at me. We both stare into each other's eyes. I could spend every waking minute staring into those eyes. Every time is like the first time. I notice my staring and quickly stand up.

"I guess that's our cue," I say, dusting the dirt off my clothes.

"Will you guys come on?" Dani yells back.

Jess and I look at each other and head back to the campsite. Dani is a bigger pain in my butt than Dakota, and she's pretty tough to beat. I understand Jess is the coolest human to ever walk the earth, but this obsession is becoming too much…but not just for me. I think Jess feels suffocated. I feel bad for her. She can't even run to me when she's sick of Dani because Dani won't let her be alone with me for two seconds. Now that I think of it, I'm ready to leave this place so me and Jess can be "best friends" in peace.

When we get back, Jason motions for Jess to come talk to him, leaving me and Dani alone. I'm searching as hard as I can for Teagan.

"Why were you guys out there when we needed to be gone?"

Oh god, she's talking to me. I look over at her. "What?"

"You heard what I said."

I stare at her for a few seconds to talk myself out of stooping to her level. I'll just rise to *a* level instead.

"What is your problem with me?" I ask.

"I don't have a problem with you."

"Dani, just be a big girl and admit that you do. And do it fast before Jess comes back," I say, checking over my shoulder just in case.

"I don't have a problem with you, Marley."

"Then what is it?"

She shakes her head in frustration. "I just think it's annoying that Jess calls you her best friend when you guys don't even hang out. She's always texting you and always talking about you. Marley this, Marley that. You guys have never hang out outside of school so I don't even get how you're considered her best friend. You didn't even come on any of the lake trips like I did."

"So? Who says hanging out outside of school defines a friendship?"

"It's just annoying."

I shake my head. "You need to get over that. Jess and I will always be best friends."

"We'll see," she says, squinting her eyes like she's already got an evil plan in place.

"What's that supposed to mean?"

"Nothing…hey, Jess!"

I turn around as Jess is approaching us. She knows something is up and is probably regretting leaving us alone together.

"Everything good with Jason?" Dani asks.

"Yeah," she replies.

The short reply has Dani uneasy. "Are you ready to find the others?"

I roll my eyes and walk off to find them. I can't take another minute of that girl. I would like to know what she meant by her "we'll see" comment. My mom has always told me not to stoop to someone's level, but Dani is definitely asking for it.

She and Jess follow as we hunt for the other three.

I return to my cabin to change out of my sweaty clothes. My phone buzzes. It's a text from David.

David (1:23pm): Just left the hospital. Been sitting with Brandon. Will talk soon, k?

Me (1:24pm): K.

I let out a sigh of relief.

All of this petty stuff with Dani seems so stupid now. I don't know what her problem is, but I'm not in the mood to play Miss Popularity. Like, seriously! We're in high school now.

Chapter 11

Ziplining was pretty awkward for me. I was in the middle of figuring out some major information about Dani and Logan when I ran into a completely different issue, to no one's surprise. Dani has once again figured out a way to irritate me to the point of no return. I try so hard to not let her get to me, which is so easy when she's not around. But as soon as she shows up, it's another story.

I pretend everything is fine so I can enjoy my time with my actual friends. On top of the Dani situation, the sensitive Dani and Logan information I'm keeping on the "D.L." is burning through my brain. I haven't confirmed anything, but something was definitely weird about it. I will be a bit disappointed if Logan likes Dani now; I guess I lost her interest after last night.

I can't do anything about it because I'm just not ready to tell her or anyone else about how I feel. I guess I've known for quite some time. I just...I don't know...thought my feelings were wrong or bad; I still kinda do. Church always has something bad to say about people who like the same sex, and growing up with church being such a big part of my life, it scares me.

I don't understand how liking someone could possibly be in the same group as someone who kills people for a living; but apparently they're pretty much the same thing, according to the Bible.

Besides that, I will say this trip has opened a door I never thought would open, so when I'm ready to walk through, I glad to know my friends will still be my friends. Hopefully, they don't think I'm into them just because they're girls, because I'm not.

"Guys, since it's our last night here, let's hang out in the tree house," Dakota says.

"I'm down!" Teagan responds. "Are y'all?"

"Sure," I say.

Jess, Dani, and Logan agreed to the plan too. We went to our cabins to shower and get ready for our "Girls Night." I'm sad tonight is our last night here. Besides the awkward moments, I've enjoyed hanging out with my friends the whole time, without school or sports getting in the way. Unfortunately, Jess and I haven't had any major one-on-one hang-out time. I blame Dani for being her shadow.

We grab some snacks and head over to the treehouse. We didn't have a backup plan if someone else was using it, so I guess we're just going to find out when we get there. The girls from Cabin F weren't ready so we left without them.

We find the treehouse empty. Teagan locks the hatch so no one else can get in. I sit on the couch making myself comfortable.

"So what are we going to do?" I ask Dakota.

She takes her drawstring backpack off. "Oh, I have some things up my sleeve."

Teagan and I look at each other because this can only mean bad news. Dakota takes what looks like a deck of cards out of the bag.

"I took these from my sister." She waves them in the air.

"What are they?" Teagan asks.

Before Dakota answers there's a knock at the hatch. We all look at each other to see who's going to answer it.

"I mean, T, you—"

"I know, I know," she says, dragging her feet to open it.

"Are you guys scared the boogeyman is coming to get you?" Dani asks, climbing in.

"That was Teagan's scary butt!" Dakota yells.

Jess follows after Dani. Her hair is still wet from her shower, and she's wearing a light blue pajama set with a soft star pattern on the pants. I catch myself staring and quickly look away so we can all play whatever card games Dakota stole from her sister. Teagan, Dani and Jess sit in the beanbag chairs in front of the couch, where I'm sitting with Dakota and Logan.

"So what's the game?" Dani asks.

"First, y'all have to agree to play the games and not be wimps...*Marley*," Dakota replies.

Oh, hell no. This has bad news written all over it. "I'm no wimp!" I lie. I am, I so very much am that wimp.

"*Right*. So? Are y'all down?"

"D, what is the game? This is crazy!" Teagan says.

"Ugh. Fine," she says, rolling her eyes. "Here."

She shows us a stack of cards labeled, *Never have I ever: 18+*.

Oh, dear god. Kill me.

"Oh, snap!" Teagan says. "Let me grab a drink!" She says like she's about to pour herself a martini or whatever they're called.

"Oh, wow," I reply. Logan, Jess, and Dani are looking at Dakota like she's insane. Because she is.

"So?!"

I shake my head. "Isn't that a game for people in college?"

"Yeah, so? I'm fifteen and you'll be fifteen in a few months. Have some fun, Marley."

"I guess we can try it out," Dani says.

"What can go wrong?" Logan chimes in.

Everything. Everything can go wrong with *this* kind of game.

Dakota puts the bag behind her. "We won't do the nasty ones! But we gotta have some fun too."

I glance at Jess because I know she wants to make a run for it. I can't help but keep shaking my head because there's no surprise this was up Dakota's sleeve.

Teagan sits back down. "So how do we start?"

"We'll play with five fingers since y'all are scared. Hold up your hands."

I can see this ending badly.

"If you lie, you're kicked out!"

"How will you know if someone's lying?" Logan asks.

"I'll know, Lo Lo."

Ugh. She has to stop calling her that.

"Marley, put your hand up!"

I slowly raise my hand with suspicion. I officially don't want to be in here. But here we go. Dakota starts.

"Never have I ever cheated on a test."

That's the question? Oh, this may not be so bad.

Everyone put a finger down except for Dani and Jess.

Jess gives me a surprised look as she sees her best friend is not the flawless person she thought I was. Yes, I'm bad news, Jess.

I chuckle. "Hey, it wasn't my fault! My eyes...um, wandered."

We laugh. Dakota places the card down and grabs another one.

"Never have I ever thought a teacher was cute."

My mind immediately went back to elementary school. My P.E. teacher was extremely attractive. But, for obvious reasons, I cannot put a finger down because my P.E. teacher was, in fact, a woman.

Everyone puts a finger down except for me. Bad play, Marley Waters.

"What?! Marley no way you haven't thought *one* teacher was cute!" Dani says.

"Yeah, Mar! What about Mr. Freddy in sixth grade?! Woo, that man was delish!" Teagan says, pretending to drool.

"Oh, um, yeah I guess so. I forgot about him."

"See? Put a finger down!"

I put my finger down, but not for Mr. Freddy. "All right, what's next?"

Dakota picks up the next card. "Never have I ever..." she looks up at us and pauses. We all stare. Teagan's nodding her head as if to say, "Go on."

"What?" I ask.

"Sorry, Lo Lo," she says nervously. "Never have I ever... kissed a girl."

And there it is. I avoid glancing at Jess, whom I know has kissed a girl, only no one knows that but me. And that also means Dani has kissed a girl too. I wonder if they're going to put their fingers down. This is so going to make things awkward for those two BFFs.

Logan grins. "I've never kissed a girl, Dakota."

"Wait, what? I thought you like girls?"

"I do. I've just never kissed one."

"Oh, shit. My bad!"

"It's okay."

As Dakota and Teagan start grilling Logan for more info, I sneak a glance at Jess, who's picking at her fingers. Dani seems interested in the conversation they're having with Logan, so I don't think she's too bothered. Jess looks up at me, and I panic and look away. We haven't spoken of the kiss since that night at the dance. It's like we tucked it away in a bottle and threw it out to sea, never to see it again. Something tells me she and Dani haven't brought it up either.

The question also has me wondering…Logan's never kissed a girl? I thought she and Dani might've kissed or something when they were being weirdos in the cabin… maybe not. This trip has become so confusing, I can't stand it. I think I'm ready to go home.

"We're gonna find you a girl, Lo Lo. Do we know any girls who like girls?" Dakota says, eyeing the group for an answer.

I quickly shake my head no.

"Um, there are those two girls who were dating when we were in seventh grade, but they're sophomores this year," Teagan adds. "Don't worry Lo Lo, we'll be the best wing-women!"

Logan laughs. "You guys don't have to find someone for me."

"Why not? Don't you want a girlfriend?" Teagan asks.

"I mean, yes, but, I've never had one or know what it's like. I just know I like girls. Kind of like you know you like boys."

Dakota leans into Logan. "I'll switch teams for you, boo."

Laughing, Logan replies, "I don't think it works like that."

Everyone chuckles, and we move on.

"Okay, next one," Dakota, says.

"Wait, do you guys hear that?" Teagan ask.

I glance at her. "Hear what?"

"Hold on."

She gets up and walks to the window. "Oh. My. GOD!" she yells.

"What's happening?" Dani asks.

"Water balloon fight! Let's go!" she says, rushing for the hatch. She opens it and climbs down like a fire fighter responding to a fire.

"Well, I guess that's that," I say, getting off the couch.

"Wait for me, T!" Dakota yells.

Dani and Jess shrug and make their way to the exit. Logan follows behind them. I grab Dakota's cards and put them back in her bag. The last thing we need is bullhorn Taebor finding out we've been playing this.

"You coming?"

I look toward the hatch; Logan is holding it open for me. "Yeah, I was just looking for somewhere to hide this."

"Want some help?"

"Oh...um, sure."

She comes back inside and the hatch door slams shut. "Sorry."

I laugh. "No biggie; someone will just think you shot me."

She grins. "Not funny."

"You're smiling."

"Whatever."

I smirk. "So where should we hide this?"

She examines the room. "What about here?" She points behind the couch.

"I don't know. That doesn't seem very discreet."

"Here," she says, taking the bag out of my hand. "I'll show you where."

I follow her over to the couch. She unzips the couch. Who knew it could even do that?! Not me! Logan stuffs the bag, literally, inside the couch.

"I didn't even know that was a thing," I say.

"You learn something new every day."

"Very true."

Her faces goes from a light smile to a frown. Did I say something wrong? I'm always upsetting someone!

"You okay?"

"Not really."

I sit on the couch. "What's wrong?"

She begins pacing. "Earlier…it's not what you think."

"What do you mean? At your cabin?"

"Yeah."

She glances at the hatch. I'm guessing she's hoping no one busts in. I'm trying to make sure my heart doesn't burst out of my chest. I have no idea what I'm about to hear.

"Okay?" I reply.

"I can't say why I was being weird, but it wasn't because of anything you've probably thinking since then."

I raise my eyebrows. "I wasn't thinking any—"

"Marley."

"Yeah?"

"I know you're lying. You've avoided looking at me all day."

Well, I do that anyway, but I'm not about to throw myself under the bus.

"Me?"

She rolls her eyes. "Have you ever liked someone, but it was impossible for you to be with them?"

I freeze. I try to say words, but words aren't coming out; my specialty. My mind immediately pictures Jess; I can't tell her that, though. The confusing thing is Logan is really cool too, so I'm stuck. I feel like I'm in that Hannah Montana episode where Miley can't choose between Jake and Jesse.

"Um—" I start. Logan cuts me off.

"I like you."

My mouth falls open and I realize now I'm staring at her.

"If would have known I'd be walking on that bus and meeting you, I would have saved myself the heartache. I think you're so funny and sweet."

I'm still staring.

"I don't want to freak you out since I'm obviously a girl, but I can't hold this in anymore. I can't have you thinking I'm into Dani. Because I'm not."

I'm seriously speechless.

"Please don't hate me."

I'm dumbfounded. I didn't actually believe Logan was into me, but she actually is. What. The. Hell. What do I do?! I'm not ready, but she is beyond beautiful and I'm definitely attracted to her.

"I don't hate you. That would be pretty shallow of me, don't you think?"

Her eyes water. "Some people get freaked out when someone of the same sex likes them."

"I'm not some people."

She sniffs. "Trust me, I know."

"Don't cry," I say, walking over to her. I put my right arm around her shoulders; she's a few inches shorter than me so she fits like a glove as I hug her.

"I swear I won't tell the others."

"I'm not embarrassed that you like me, Logan."

Truth is, I wish I wasn't afraid to be myself. I'm trying to fight my feelings because I'm scared my family will send me off to some conversion camp or reject me forever. I've been struggling with this for two years.

We let go. "You wanna go throw some water balloons at my face?"

She smiles and pats my cheek. "I don't want to mess up this pretty little face."

I laugh and walk toward the hatch.

We leave and join the others. I'm feeling so many emotions as I run around the campground ducking flying water balloons. Logan telling me she likes me replays in my head a million times, but I also can't stop thinking about Jess. What will she think? What if Logan tells them she likes me? Oh god, my stomach feels funny.

"Marley? What are you doing? This is no time to daydream! Run!" Teagan yells as a mob of boys chases her toward me.

My friends, Cameron and Josh are leading the pack with their arms cocked and ready to throw. Snapping out of it, my eyes grow wide and I take off running. I don't get too far when I feel a balloon splatter against my back. I fall to the ground over dramatically, like I've been shot. Teagan trips over me and falls. The mob of boys unleash the rest of their arsenal of water balloons on us.

"Ah!" I squeal.

"All right, all right, you got us!" Teagan yells. They cease fire.

"There's Jason! Let's get him!" Cameron yells. They update their target to Jason and take off.

"I'm soaked," I say to Teagan, wringing out my shirt.

She pats the side of her head. "I know, I think there's water in my ear."

I laugh. "Thank you for bringing them toward me, punk."

"Hey, I needed help!"

"What was I going to do against a mob of those boys?"

"You had a balloon! I thought maybe you'd throw it. Why didn't you? Why were you just standing there?" she asks.

I don't know how to answer her question so I shrug my shoulders.

"Are you okay?"

"Yeah...."

"Hmm."

"What? Teagan, stop. I'm fine."

"Whatever you say, Mar."

I stand. "Let's go find the others."

Teagan and I take off on our search. It's not easy looking for your friends while hundreds of other kids are running around screaming. I'm glad T didn't pry any further, I had no exit strategy to get out of that conversation.

"There's Jess and Dani. Let's see what they're doing," Teagan says, pointing.

I get nervous, wondering if Jess has already heard the news that Logan likes me. I'm surprised I haven't grown gray hair with all the stress I'm putting myself through.

"Sup guys?" Teagan says as we walk up.

"Hey, we've been looking for y'all," Jess replies.

"We have?" Dani adds.

Teagan and I glance at Dani. I look at Jess with my best "I told you so" face. She never listens to me. "What's got your panties in a bunch?" Teagan asks.

"Nothing."

"Hey, can we talk real quick?" Jess asks me.

That's weird. What would she want to talk about?

"Really, Jess? We're supposed to go grab s'mores," Dani says while she's glaring at me.

I'm keeping calm for Jess. Ugh, she completely has me wrapped around her little finger.

"We'll be five minutes, Dani. Geez."

A frown forms on Dani's face. I look at Jess in shock. I've never heard her talk to Dani like that before. Was it because of our chat from earlier? Either way, thank god! Jess putting on her big girl pants is pretty attractive. Per usual, Teagan is watching like it's an episode of *Bad Girls Club*.

"Dani, come hang with me and we can go find Dakota and Logan," Teagan finally says, reaching for Dani's arm.

She jerks it back. "I don't want to go find them."

Jess and I stare at her. "What the hell is wrong with you?" I ask. I can't hold my tongue anymore. She's off the charts today.

"You're my problem, Marley!"

"Whoa," Teagan says, moving closer to me. My heart gathers speed. I hate confrontation. It gives me anxiety.

"Okay and why is that?" I ask, folding my arms. Teagan is now glaring at her.

Dani's skin is flushed. She probably feels like we're ganging up on her.

She lets out a sigh. "Forget it. We can go find them."

"No, no," Teagan says. "Say what you have to say, Dani."

I glance at Jess. I know she's uncomfortable.

"You're just not as innocent as you make it seem."

I look at Teagan. My face scrunches into confusion. "Again, what the hell are you talking about?" I ask.

"Dani, you need to take a breather. I don't like where this is going for you," Teagan says. You can see the anger lasers getting ready to shoot from her eyes.

"Marley," Jess says, grabbing my arm. I wipe her hand away. Dani is standing there like she's negotiating in her head what she's going to say next.

"Jess thinks you're this awesome best friend, but you're not. You keep secrets from her—an actual best friend doesn't do that."

Jess frowns and looks at me. "What is she talking about?"

"I have no idea," I reply.

"Spit it out, Danielle!" Teagan shrieks.

I've never heard anyone call Dani by her real name. She really has Teagan pissed off.

I know for a fact that not a single person on this planet knows how I feel about Jess; but for some reason I can't help but to think that's what Dani's talking about. I'm going to barf.

"What secrets?" I ask.

Dani glances at us three one-by-one before spilling her news. "You never told Jess that Logan *like likes* you."

I feel Teagan and Jess swiftly turn their heads toward me.

"Logan likes you?" Jess asks. I look at her and she's staring into my eyes. I'm in such a state of shock I can't respond.

Teagan starts, "Logan likes—wait…" she turns to Dani. "Why would you do that? *Especially* after Taylor P was just crucified by the entire freshman class for being an idiot."

Teagan continues lecturing Dani. I wasn't going to say anything to anyone about Logan having feelings for me. I was going to leave it up to her to disclose. Jess is watching everything unfold and something tells me she's not happy.

I find myself stepping toward Dani. My jaw tightens. I want to shove her to the ground, but I can hear Mom in my ear. Plus, I don't think my new basketball coach would put someone who's violent on the varsity team.

"You know what? I say glaring into her eyes. "You aren't worth it." I storm past her, bumping into her shoulder – but not too hard because well…Jess.

"Marley!" Jess yells, grabbing my hand. She pulls me back. "Stop walking."

"What Jess?"

"I'm sorry for that. I don't know why she's acting all weird like that."

"Jess, I'm sick of this." I start. "Ever since you, *you know*, she hasn't been the same. She's been after me for two years and I can't be around her anymore. I'm done." I take off walking again.

"Marley, will you stop?!" she says, stepping in front of me.

I let out a sigh.

"Ever since I what?"

I look around to make sure no one is within listening distance. "Ever since…ever since you kissed her."

We haven't spoken of the kiss since the night of the dance. Her head drops to the ground. I sigh. "I'm sorry I didn't—"

"Why didn't you tell me about Logan?" she asks.

I feel flustered. "Jess, I just found out like forty-five minutes ago. I haven't seen you since we left the treehouse. I wasn't even going to tell anyone."

She looks up, "Oh…okay. Great, Marley. So, we do keep secrets. Dani is right. I told you my deepest darkest secret and you already made up your mind you weren't telling me yours."

"Dani is what? Jess that's not fair. And this is definitely not my deepest darkest secret."

"It's clear you don't trust me," she says, glancing down at the ground.

What is happening? This trip has been a gift from hell. Dani is officially dead to me.

"Jess."

Teagan marches up to us. "Jess, I'm sorry but I kicked Dani out of our group and she's not allowed in our cabin anymore."

Jess looks at us in shock and looks behind her, I'm assuming, to see where Dani is. "I should go check on her," she says.

I chuckle. "Sure Jess, go to your best friend," I say and walk away. I turn around once more. "She can do no wrong, right?" I grin and shake my head. I turn around and head for the cabin. I'm done for the night.

On the way, I pass Dakota and Logan.

"Marley!" Dakota yells.

I ignore her and continue walking. I don't make it five more steps before I'm pulled back abruptly. "Ow," I say.

"What the hell? I was calling your name," Dakota says. Logan catches up, but she's watching D. I'm assuming to avoid eye contact with me.

I sigh. "Not right now, D. I'm going to bed."

"Bed? It's eight o'clock and it's our last night here. You're not going to bed."

"I am."

"Okay, what's wrong?" she asks, sounding genuinely concerned.

"Nothing."

"Marley."

"I'm serious. I have a headache. I'm tired."

She turns around. "Teagan!" she yells at the top of her lungs. Is this a dream? This can't really be my life. I roll my eyes at Dakota as Teagan jogs over.

"There you are, Mar! I was trying to find you after I told Jess off."

"You told Jess off? Saying what?" This can't be good.

"I told her she needs to choose."

"Choose? Choose what?"

"Yeah, choose what?" Dakota echoes.

"To be friends with Dani or Marley. Dani is a bitch!"

"Okay, what in the hell did we miss?" Dakota asks.

Logan's eyes widen. "You gave Jess an ultimatum?"

Teagan's face curls. "A what?"

"An ultimatum. It's like choosing one or the other and both have consequences."

"Oh! Yeah, I sure did."

There's way too much to take in right now. I'm learning Teagan has now put the fate of my favorite person in the world at stake. As pissed off as I am at Jess, we usually talk it out; maybe not this time. Dani crossed the line. I'm curious to see if she actually does choose Dani over me. I think my heart will shatter.

Chapter 12

L ast night is officially rated the worst night of my life. I wake to a throbbing headache. I remember I didn't take the pills Logan gave me on day one so I search through my pockets. Gross, I know, but I'm desperate.

After we updated Dakota and Logan on what happened we all decided to chill in the cabin and watch Mean Girls for our last night's hoorah. Logan wasn't too pleased to hear Dani outed her secret. She also told us that was part of the reason why she and Dani were in the cabin together. At the time, she couldn't tell me why, apparently Logan decided to tell Dani a secret in return for the one Dani had told her.

Logan never told me Dani's secret. I'm glad someone knows how to keep one around here. Though, I'm pretty sure I already know what it's about. I'm assuming Dani kept her secret from Teagan and Dakota so they wouldn't start asking all sorts of weird and awkward questions.

The end-of-camp volleyball game is after breakfast and then we'll load the buses and head home. This has been one hell of a trip. I'm beyond exhausted. I get dressed and head to the mess hall. I browse through the food options, but the more I search, the less I want to eat.

I grab an apple and a water bottle and sit at a table in the corner of the building. I take a bite of the apple so I can take a pill for this raging headache. Mom says I need to have food in my stomach before I throw medicine into my body. I hope an apple counts.

I'm thinking about Brandon, Jess, and Logan, but Jess is completely outweighing the others because of Teagan's big ultimatum show. I can't believe she did that, but I can't be mad at her for protecting me. She's being a best friend and I appreciate that.

Jess comes into the mess hall. I sink low in my seat, hoping to blend in with the wall. I look around for Dani, but I don't see her. Did she not choose her?

I feel like a stalker as I watch her grab breakfast. Should I speak to her? Does this mean I won? Jess grabs an orange juice bottle and looks for a table. Her eyes scan over to where I'm sitting. I sink lower. I have no idea if she saw me but I'm going to pretend she didn't.

My eyes wander over to the mess hall doors and Dani walks in. Uh oh. Here we go. I see Jess is sitting with Jason and his friends. I lock back onto Dani to see what she does. She grabs her breakfast and makes her way through the mess hall. I'm watching her every move.

My phone buzzes. It's David letting me know he's doing a little better today. I tell him I'll call him when I get home later today.

I look back up, remembering I'm on a stake-out. Dani's gone. She's not in mess hall anymore. Jess is still eating with

Jason and his crew. Did I actually win this ultimatum? Did Jess really pick me? I finish my apple, trying not to get ahead of myself. Oh, who am I kidding, I'm so happy right now.

I get up to toss the apple core and water bottle. I make my way to Jess; we should probably talk about last night. I nervously make my way across the room. I tap her on her shoulder. "Hey, can we talk?"

She turns around. "No."

Well…that was unexpected. "No?"

"Yes, no."

"Why not?"

"Because I have nothing to say to you."

My heart sinks. In the two years of knowing Jess, she's never looked at me the way she is right now. "Give me two minutes."

She slides out of the chair and walks over by the window. "Before you—"

"I'll start," she says. "I'll give this conversation ten seconds. I've been friends with Dani since I was seven years old, and I know what she did was wrong but for you to make me choose between you two was totally wrong. You had Teagan yelling in my face for something I didn't do. I was trying to change for you. I was going to tell Dani myself that she needed to cut it out with you or I was done with her – but no. Instead, you get Teagan to yell in my face, giving me that stupid ultimatum. I don't know who you are anymore. And I can't be friends with someone who gives me an ultimatum. And the only reason I know you agreed to it is because you didn't text me yourself so we could talk about it last night."

I feel a lump in my throat, my eyes are flooding with tears.

She continues, "And for the record, I choose neither of you. Bye, Marley."

As she walks off a tear falls down my cheek. It feels like I just got news of someone dying.

∽

I decide not to play volleyball. My ankle is still bothering me and I'm in the worst mood imaginable. I don't want to talk to anyone. I want to go home. Everything you could possibly think of has gone wrong on this trip. Did I forget to eat my black-eyed peas this year?

I watch the game from my cabin steps. I don't care who wins. Teagan and Dakota are playing. I have no idea where Logan is. I could care even less about where Dani might be. I haven't seen Jess since the mess hall.

Why did I beg Mom to let me come on this trip? I shouldn't have cleaned my room like we agreed. I should have just gone to bingo with my grandma. I'd still have my best friend if I did that. Every time I think of Jess, I want to cry. I can't stop seeing the disappointment on her face. I really want to be mad at Teagan. But I can't.

I go inside to lay across my bed. I call my mom to let her know we're leaving soon and to let dad know. I don't feel like making another phone call. I must have fallen asleep because I'm woken to loud cheers coming into the cabin.

"Woo! Mar, we won!" Teagan exclaims.

I open one eye, my head is still throbbing.

"Marley, pack up your stuff. Time to go," Dakota says, zipping her bag.

I crawl out of bed like a zombie and pack my bag. I don't speak again until we head out. Teagan's afraid to talk to me because she feels like it's her fault Jess dumped me. It's not, I mean, it kinda…ugh, I don't know.

Taebor is outside giving us her last blasts of her beloved bullhorn. I pray she doesn't carry that thing around at school. As I walk towards the stairway to heaven, I hear my name behind me. It's Logan.

"Hey, do you mind helping me with my bag again?"

"Sure," I reply. "Um, is—"

"No, they're already on the bus," she grins.

"Great," I say as I walk up the steps.

I grab her bag and adjust it so I can carry it with mine.

"Teagan told me about this morning. I'm sorry. Who needs her?"

"Who's her?"

"Jess. She's cute but a bad friend."

My face twisted, "Jess is not a bad friend."

"Right. I watched her just let Dani be rude to you for three full days."

"I really don't feel like talking about this, Logan." I head for the door.

"Fine," she says. "Just so you know, I meant what I said."

I turn around, "What did you say?"

"When I told you I like you. You're always so tense, I'd totally chill you out since I'm always so happy."

I'm not tense? Am I? I know I overthink, like David said, but I don't think I'd call it tense.

"I'm not tense. I'm just frustrated. It's been a long few days."

"Okay."

"Let's go before they leave us stranded. I'm convinced this place is cursed. I just want to get the hell out of here."

We begin to head for the door again.

"Wait," Logan says, pulling me back. She gently places her right hand on my cheek. Her eyes fall to my lips and she pulls our bodies close. My heart is definitely exceeding the number of beats per minute that constitutes as safe – I think I'm experiencing cardiac arrest.

She draws my head in closer, bringing my lips closer to hers. I'm four seconds away from passing out.

"Tell me to stop if my radar was wrong," she says as her eyes stare deep into mine. The English language has left the building; I am brain dead. She leans in and her lips connect with mine, sending electric butterflies throughout my body.

My hands are awkwardly weighed down by my sides – I was so not ready to be kissed today…*especially* by a girl!

I quickly pull away and stare at her. My heart is still pounding through my shirt.

"I'm sorry," she says. "I shouldn't have done that."

The door creaks and my neck swings over.

Jess is standing in the doorway…